D0438813

PRETTIEST DOLL

by Gina Willner-Pardo

Clarion Books
Houghton Mifflin Harcourt
New York • Boston • 2012

Clarion Books
215 Park Avenue South, New York, New York 10003

Clarion Books is an imprint of Houghton Mifflin Harcourt Publishing Company.

www.hmhbooks.com

The text was set in 13-point Norlik.

Library of Congress Cataloging-in-Publication Data
Willner-Pardo, Gina.
Prettiest doll / by Gina Willner-Pardo.
p. cm.
Summary: A beauty contestant since she was three, Olivia, now thirteen, has begun feeling limited by her beauty, but a shared journey with Danny, a boy struggling with his own appearance, shows her she has choices and resources beyond her appearance.
ISBN 978-0-547-68170-2 (hardcover)
[1. Beauty contests—Fiction. 2. Beauty, Personal—Fiction. 3. Mothers and daughters—Fiction. 4. Self-perception—Fiction. 5. Runaways—Fiction.] I. Title.
PZ7.W6856Pre 2012
[Fic]—dc23
2011042315
Manufactured in the United States of America
DOC 10 9 8 7 6 5 4 3 2 1
4500380132

For Evan and Cara. And for Robert,
who took me to Missouri.

one

IT'S good to be pretty. I'm really lucky.

I have blond hair that's usually straight, but I can make it wavy with a curling iron or hot rollers. Not everyone's hair holds a curl, but mine does. And I have brown eyes and straight white teeth and a smile that's not too much gum. My mom says that if I'd needed braces, she'd have found a way, but thank the good Lord I never did. She says it would be better if my eyes were blue, though.

So I'm lucky. But sometimes, when I should be feeling lucky, I don't. Sometimes, if I really pay attention, it's like there are other feelings inside me, buried down deep, close but far away. It scares me a little, but then I remember about my hair.

I did my first pageant when I was three. Mama thought doing pageants would give me poise. The one we started with was Missouri's Sweetest Angel, and I came in fourth in the Pee Wee division. Amber Dickerson pinched me backstage to make me cry and even though I stopped before I had to go out, you could see that my mascara was smeared. Amber came in second. I would have won if she hadn't made me cry. Mama always says, "That Amber Dickerson is a piece of work." Then I forget who I'm talking to and say, "She's a bitch," and Mama says, "Olivia Jane, that's not how you been raised."

I keep my mouth shut then, but it doesn't change my mind. I'm thirteen now, so I've known Amber for ten years, and she's been a bitch all along. I'm not the only one who thinks so. Imogene Boggs, who is my best friend and who is into horses, not pageants, always says that if there was an award like Miss Congeniality, only for being mean, Amber would win it.

I don't know what I would do without Imogene. We are nothing alike on the outside. She is tall and has thin brown hair that she wears in a sloppy ponytail. I feel sorry for her about her hair, but she doesn't care. The main thing she cares about is her horse, Honey. She goes out to the stables every day after school. Sometimes I go with her, but I have to be careful about the mud on account of Mama not liking me to track it into the house. Imogene wears riding boots and says she doesn't even notice the mud. It's amazing how different two people who are best friends can be.

"You should take riding lessons instead," she said

when I told her how much I dreaded singing at Prettiest Doll, the next big pageant I was practicing for.

We were in Honey's stall, watching as Honey took a big, slurping drink of water from her trough. The day was warm, the way it is once in a while before Thanksgiving and frost. The trees around the barn were bare, but the air still smelled a little like wet leaves mixed with hay and horse and the sun about to start going down.

"Can't. It's too much money," I said.

"I could teach you. For free. So we could hang out."

Imogene is like that. I love her so much.

I thought about what it would be like to be at the stables every day, tending to Honey, riding the trails, laughing with Imogene.

"I've got to have a talent for pageants," I said. "You can't ride a horse for your talent. You have to sing or dance or play piano or twirl a baton. You can't bring a horse in there."

"It'd be funny, though, wouldn't it? Leading a horse out on that stage? All the moms going crazy?" Imogene grabbed the rubber curry and began to loosen the dirt on Honey's neck.

I let myself smile a little, imagining. But just a little, because thinking about it too much made me think even more about the singing and how much I hated it, how I was boxed in.

"I don't see why it has to be singing," I said. "It's the one thing I'm terrible at."

"Tell your mama," Imogene said. "She'll let you do something else."

"You know how she is."

"She wants you to win, doesn't she?"

I watched Imogene brushing Honey's neck, pushing the curry in perfect-size circles, knowing just how to do it right.

"I don't see what we have to have a talent for, anyway," I said. "Everyone knows it's mainly about how you look."

Imogene nodded, still focusing on what she was doing.

"Well, you got that part sewed up tight," she said. "You're always the prettiest one."

She said it as though she really thought so and wasn't jealous at all, not like Jenna and Marlena, our other friends at school, who have a way of paying you a compliment that sounds like they really wished you'd get hit by a bus.

Honey flicked her tail at a fly. She stomped her rear hoof, and a little cloud of dust rose around her.

"It's okay, girl," Imogene whispered, rubbing her side. "Shhh."

"You know just how to calm her down," I said after a minute. "You're a horse whisperer."

Imogene leaned her cheek forward and rested it against Honey's neck, not even minding the dirt.

"It's a feeling," she said. "It's like you're talking without words. Like words would get in the way, almost."

Sometimes Imogene gets all dramatic about horses.

There was silence in the barn. All I could hear was a jay cawing. I watched Imogene leaning against Honey. Maybe they were talking in some wordless way. I don't know. To me it looked like nothing was happening. It made me think that riding horses would be something I wouldn't be very good at.

Imogene went back to brushing. Honey snorted. The sun had lowered itself again and was shining through the open side of the stall, directly at me, making me sweat, which I hated. I slid myself over a little along the rail until I was back in the shade.

"What are you going to wear?" Imogene asked.

"A dress I already have for Talent. Green satin, with a pouffy skirt. And for Beauty, a new one. With a burgundy top."

"Burgundy's red, right?" Imogene asked. When

I nodded yes, she said, "Burgundy goes good with brown eyes."

Judges really like the girls with blue eyes. Amber Dickerson's have little yellow flecks in them.

"You have pretty eyes, Liv," Imogene said.

"I wish I was taller," I said, to get myself to stop thinking about Amber. "I wish I was tall and slim like you."

Imogene doesn't have to think at all about what she eats. She could probably be in pageants if she wanted to.

She shrugged, running the brush down Honey's side.

"You're tall enough," she said. "You're perfect. No wonder you always win." She paused for a moment. "But you'd be good at riding, too, if you gave it a chance. You know that, right?"

It was like she was a friend whisperer, too.

"I wish you could do something just for the fun of it once in a while," she said.

"Well, I can't," I said. It came out harsher than I meant it. "So how am I going to get out of singing in front of all those people?"

"Well, you like dancing, right? Tell her if she lets you do dancing instead of singing, you'll practice harder."

"She says all the judges are tired of seeing me dance. She says I have to wow them with something new."

I've been dancing since I was three. Miss Denise,

who is my pageant coach when she's not being a hairdresser, says I have to hold my head up and remember about pointing my toes.

"And baton twirling is out," I said, thinking of all the times I'd dropped the baton Mama got me for Christmas one year. "I hate that dang baton."

"What else is there besides singing and dancing and baton twirling?"

"Nothing. That's it."

"What about painting a picture? Or writing a poem?"

"It has to be talent you can do on a stage," I said.

Besides, I'm not good at writing or art. I'm not good at anything except being pretty. Mama says being pretty is the best thing to be good at because that's what people really care about. "Being pretty is what opens doors," she says.

I'm really lucky.

We live in Luthers Bridge, which doesn't have an apostrophe because the government says apostrophes are confusing in place names and only makes a few exceptions, like Martha's Vineyard. We learned this in third grade.

Luthers Bridge is famous for apple butter and having more churches than any other town in southwest Missouri. Ours is New Faith Gospel. There used to be an actual Luther's Bridge, but it got torn down in the fifties to make room for the high school. I don't know who Luther was.

Luthers Bridge is in the foothills of the Ozark Mountains. Most of the people who live here have lived here all their lives. The people who want to go get the hell out fast. Mama says there were fifty-eight kids in her class at Horace Widener High School and thirty-six of them left the summer after graduation. Most of them didn't go far: Kansas City or St. Louis or Columbia, where the university is, which everyone calls Mizzou. But they didn't come back, except to visit. That left twenty-two kids, including Mama and Daddy. They got engaged under the Fourth of July fireworks that year. They didn't even think about leaving because Daddy had a job at the Dollar General. That was before he started driving semis for Smaker Brothers Trucking, leaving Mama alone all the time to take care of me. She always says they were heading for divorce and probably would have gotten one if Daddy hadn't been in that awful wreck and died.

He died in Georgia, on Interstate 475, right by the side of the road, before the ambulance could even get there. And about the second he died, his brother, Fred, up and left Luthers Bridge to go live in Chicago.

So that was the two men I loved just gone, all of a sudden.

Even if they were going to get divorced, Mama still feels bad about Daddy. I know she does. She doesn't talk about him much, but she has four pictures of him in the dining room, over the china cabinet. She says those pictures are for me, so I don't forget. Once I asked if I could hang them up in my room and she said there were already holes in the dining room wall, so no.

Sometimes I practice for pageants in the dining room. There's space to work on my walk and my twirls. Sometimes I pretend it's Mama and Daddy both watching me. I try to smile extra big, the way I think I would always smile if I had a father who came to pageants. It's funny how many fathers don't. It's mostly moms who come.

It was almost five when I got home from Imogene's. I took off my Vans and left them on the front steps so I wouldn't get mud in the house. Mud really sets Mama's teeth on edge.

"Where you been?" she called from the kitchen as I closed the front door.

"Imogene's. I told you."

"No, you did not."

"I *did*."

"Well, then how come I thought we were going to practice? How come I took off an hour early? Which I *know* I told you about."

Mama works weekdays at Creech's Bakery, baking cakes for Jim and Carol-Ann Creech, who were two years ahead of her in high school. Jim is pretty nice to work for, but Carol-Ann doesn't like Mama taking off extra time.

"Don't even *think* about telling me you didn't know," Mama was saying.

In her spare time, when she's not working with me on pageant stuff, Mama does taxidermy, which means she stuffs dead animals and makes them look alive again. It was Grandpa's business, and Mama grew up just knowing how to do it. When Grandpa died, Mama took it over. She does it at Grandma's, fortunately, so we don't have dead animals lying around. There are billboards all over southwestern Missouri saying TAXIDERMY BY ROY, with Grandpa's phone number on them. Thank the good Lord it's not our phone number, or the kids at school might figure it out. I've never told anyone except Imogene. Something about Mama stuffing dead caribou makes me feel ashamed. Mama says she doesn't mind, though. She says you get used to it, and also that it's fun, making dead things look pretty again.

"Get your butt in here, Olivia Jane," Mama called from the kitchen.

Mama's a big woman, but she didn't used to be. When she was my age, she was skinny as a rail. "And

I ate everything, Olivia Jane," she always says. "Didn't matter what I ate. I was all knees and elbows." She has pictures of herself to prove it.

She has blond hair like I do, but she perms it. Perms are old-fashioned and also bad for your hair. Mama's hair would look better straight, but she got used to perming it when she was a teenager and can't stop. I wonder if it'll be like that for me, if I'll get used to doing things one way and then keep doing them even after it's not in style anymore. I bet my kids will roll their eyes when I'm not looking.

Mama was sitting at the kitchen counter looking at cookbooks. I knew without her saying anything that she was looking at cake recipes. She likes seeing how different cookbooks tell you to do different things. She likes changing her favorite cake recipes to make them more her own. Mama is definitely a perfectionist when it comes to cakes.

"Olivia Jane, just look at yourself!" Mama said, peering at me over her reading glasses.

I looked down at my black hoodie and jeans and black socks. I looked fine to myself.

"How you gonna practice in jeans?" Mama said.

"I just got home. I haven't had time to change yet."

"Well, get a move on!"

I could hear her grumbling as I rounded the corner

and headed down the hall to my room. Saying things like "Honestly!" and "I ain't got all day!" Which made me feel bad, because Mama does work hard, harder than just about anybody else's mama I know. Still, I knew it wasn't being tired or rushed that was making her grumpy. It was just the sight of me: stick-straight hair, plain jeans, no bright colors, nails without polish, no false eyelashes or mascara. It's hard for Mama to look at me when I look like everyone else. She won't admit it, but I know it's true.

The afternoon sun was almost gone, but my room was still hot. I slid open my window a crack for breeze. Then I went to the closet and pulled out my pageant evening wear. Mama bought it new off eBay. "That's a pronghorn antelope just for you," she said when the box arrived in the mail. I knew that meant the dress had cost five hundred dollars, which is what Mama charges for some of the big game and exotic sheep.

I held the dress against me and looked in my mirror. It was a pretty dress. I'll say that. A burgundy satin bodice, sleeveless, to show off my nice arms. And a burgundy sash with a removable flower. We'd probably keep the flower on. It was more feminine that way, Mama said. The skirt was tea length, white with four layers: white satin attached to a netting for fullness, another layer of white satin, and then two layers of fluffy white tulle. The outside layer had delicate burgundy flowers sewn all around. And the whole thing came with matching burgundy satin gloves and a hair band with a crown of burgundy flowers and burgundy and pink ribbons down the back.

Mama says burgundy is a good color because it makes the judges think of Christmas.

I stared at myself behind the dress, imagining what it would look like on. Even when I heard Mama calling, I just kept staring. Then, finally, when I knew I couldn't put it off anymore, I slipped out of my jeans, unzipped my hoodie, and stepped into the skirt. The satin felt cool against my skin. The netting was stiff and crinkly, like tissue paper.

Then I stared at myself in the mirror some more. It was the weirdest thing. I wasn't there. I had disappeared. Suddenly I couldn't catch my breath. It was like being underwater or buried in the ground, the feeling I had—that I was invisible, that I could scream and no one would hear.

"Olivia Jane, for Lord's *sake!*" Mama called.

I stared and stared. All I could see were burgundy flowers and folds of white tulle, like a snowy field. I felt fear and anger surging through me, and all I could think was that I was in there somewhere, under all that snow, and somehow I had to get out.

two

LIKE this," Mama said. "Like this."

She stood where the kitchen blends into the dining room, arms carefully at her sides. I could tell that, in her head, she was wearing a gown with petticoats and tulle, and gloves, and maybe diamond earrings, which I knew she'd always wanted. She was not thinking of herself in her blue sweatpants and faded pink Creech's Bakery T-shirt.

"Careful steps, like this," Mama said. "And smile. *Smile.*"

We'd done this a million times before. Maybe two million. I knew all about pageant walking and twirling.

"And then you stop, like this. And then put your foot here. You see? Just like this." Mama waited until I looked down at her feet. She was barefoot. Her toenails were yellow and cracked and unpolished, because she was too fat to bend forward to paint them.

"And then you turn. Like this. Smiling the whole time. Over this shoulder and then over this one. Like this. See?"

I sighed. I couldn't help it.

"Well, you're so dang smart, I guess you don't need any help from me!" Mama sounded mad, but I knew she wasn't. She just wanted me to want to watch her.

"We've done it so many times!"

"Not *right,*" she said, lowering herself onto one of the chairs. "Don't matter how many times you do it if none of them's right."

"If I do it one more time, can we please eat?" I was so tired. And I still had homework.

"One time *right,*" she said.

I hauled myself up to standing. The netting on my dress was making me itchy. And I was afraid that maybe I was sweating and getting stains under the armholes.

I went into the kitchen and stood where she could see me from the dining room. I remembered to stand tall and smile. My smile felt fake and pasted on, but Mama was nodding.

"You're just so pretty, Olivia Jane," she said, all dreamy for a second. Then something in her face hardened up. "Now go," she said.

I walked carefully, thinking of my arms, my feet, my straight back. Smiling. Looking over my right shoulder, then flipping my head around and looking over my left. Still smiling. Or I thought I was, anyway.

Mama nodded.

"A little stiff. You want to look relaxed," she said.

"I *am* relaxed."

"Well, you look like a rubber band, all wound up," Mama said. But she pushed herself out of the chair. "Okay. Enough for now. We still got three weeks."

I felt my insides unclench. "Now can we eat?"

"Well, I gotta cook something, don't I?" She shuffled into the kitchen, opened the freezer door, and peered inside. "What do you want, baby? Pizza? Mac and cheese?"

"Pizza. And a salad."

Mama said for me to make the salad, and to make enough for just me. Without telling her, I tore off enough lettuce for both of us. And cut up an extra tomato. Mama should eat more salad.

Mama took a big bite of pizza and said, "You got Miss Denise tomorrow at four o'clock."

"I know."

"So you'll come right home after school. You won't hang out with Imogene at the barn."

"I *know*."

"And you'll practice your song tonight. After you finish your homework."

I sighed. "It sounds terrible. I sound terrible."

"That's what practicing is for, right?"

"But, Mama—"

"Olivia Jane, how many times do I have to tell you? Nobody sings good without practicing. Even the real stars practice. Even Reba. And Miss Denise is going to get you a lesson with Mrs. Elsie Drucker. She says we can squeeze in a few lessons before the pageant."

Mrs. Drucker had taught Brett-Ellis Baker, who is practically a legend in Luthers Bridge. She won every pageant there was to win in southwestern Missouri, and then, to top it all off, she came in third in Junior Miss. She got a lot of scholarship money and now she goes to Mizzou. Mama thinks Brett-Ellis Baker walks on water.

"Mama, about the singing—"

Mama closed her eyes, warding me off. "Olivia Jane, do not start with me."

"It's so expensive." Maybe that would sway her.

Mama opened her eyes and reached across the table. "It's worth every penny if it helps you be the Prettiest Doll," she said, grabbing my hand.

There was so much love in her eyes. And so much wanting. It shut me up, even though the words were right there, just ready to tumble out over my tongue.

"We need those lessons if you're going to win that crown," Mama said. "And I'll work as hard as I have to to pay for them. It don't bother me one little bit."

I hate being poor. Mama always says we shouldn't feel sorry for ourselves, because we have a house and food to eat, and that I should stop grousing. So I don't say it out loud anymore. But still.

Mama let go of my hand and straightened up a little. She picked up her half-finished slice and took a huge bite, all the way to the crust.

The next day, after school, I walked the three blocks to downtown. It was still only three thirty, so I went to Turner's for fudge.

Turner's General Store is on the town square, across from the drugstore. It's been around since my grandma was a girl, and maybe even before that. Most of the kids don't go there anymore; they'd rather get smoothies at the Bike Trail Café. Turner's doesn't have smoothies. But it has a candy case with almost every kind of candy you can think of. My favorite is the peanut butter fudge, which Merle Turner makes in the back. It's a secret recipe.

I've always loved Turner's. When I was little, I used to watch the popcorn machine while Mama shopped for fabrics and trim for my pageant costumes. I loved the dark oak walls, the narrow aisles, the bins full of buttons and ribbons and sequins and beads, the displays of plastic flowers, the shelves bulging with soft skeins of yarn. I liked walking slowly up the toy aisle, not touching the metal cars, the plastic eggs full of bandage-colored Silly Putty, jacks and little rubber balls, creepy plastic dolls with painted-on faces and tufts of coarse, uncombable hair, tiny troll figures to twist onto the eraser end of your pencil. Teachers hated those trolls.

There was a bin full of marbles, all different colors and sizes. When I was little, I couldn't resist plunging my hands into them, feeling their cool glassiness on my skin. I used to wonder what it would be like to dive down to the bottom of a swimming pool full of marbles and look up at the colors lit from behind by the sun. Could you breathe, under all those rolling balls of color and light? Would there be air down there?

I sat at the counter and Merle Turner didn't even get a menu for me. He knew what I'd be wanting.

"How was school?" he said, rummaging behind the counter for a sheet of waxed paper.

"Okay."

"You getting ready for another one of them beauty contests?"

"Yeah. But they don't call them beauty contests anymore."

"Why not?" Merle was hunting around for an extra-big hunk of fudge. He's the kind of man—tall, bald with a gray fringe, sunburned, fingers scarred up from being stuck all the time with fishhooks—who looks like the last thing he'd want to be wearing is a starched white apron, but that doesn't stop him. He has three in the back so if he gets a stain on the one he's wearing, he can switch to a clean one.

"'Cause it's not just about beauty. You have to have poise and talent."

Merle said, "So when's the next one?"

"Three weeks."

He set the fudge on a plate and put it in front of me. Then he went to the refrigerator and pulled out a little carton of milk. "You ready?"

"I guess."

He put the carton down by my plate and pulled a straw out of the jar next to the register.

"Don't sound very sure about that."

"I'm never sure at three weeks," I said. "I get surer as I go."

He laughed. "Well, Janie Tatum's sure. She says you're a shoo-in to win."

He meant Mama. I wished she wouldn't go around town talking me up.

"I don't think about winning," I said.

"Well, no harm in thinking about it." Merle set the

straw next to my plate and watched as I took a bite of fudge. "Pretty good, huh?"

I nodded, speechless with butter and sugar and peanut butter happiness.

Merle turned away, heading back to the kitchen. "Not too much of that, now. You don't want to be splitting the seams of those costumes they make you wear."

He's an old man, always nice to me. He's known me since I was a baby. I didn't say anything about how an old man shouldn't be saying anything about my weight or how I look. Because I wasn't even sure it was true. When you do pageants, it's like you're giving people permission to talk about your looks. They don't think it might be embarrassing for you. They think that's all you are.

I took a long time eating and drinking, to make the fudge last. I decided to eat only half of it. That way, I could eat the rest after Miss Denise, as a reward.

After a little while, I felt someone staring at me and slowly turned to look. Two stools down was a boy I didn't know. He was probably ten or eleven, and handsome, for a little boy. A half-finished chocolate milk shake sat in front of him. A duffel bag lay at his feet. Not a school backpack: the kind of thing you could stuff clothes into.

He was really staring.

"What?" I finally said.

"You do those weird JonBenet Ramsey things?"

JonBenet Ramsey was murdered when she was six. She did pageants. It was the first time most people had ever heard of them. She kind of gave pageants a bad name. People started connecting pageants and murder in their heads.

"You shouldn't talk about JonBenet like that," I said.

"I didn't mean *she* was weird. I mean the pageants."

He didn't talk like a ten-year-old.

"Are you from here?" I asked.

"No," he said, turning back to his milk shake. "Just passing through."

We ate for a minute in silence.

"You know, there are a lot of good things about pageants," I said.

I didn't know why I was even telling him anything. Usually, when people made nasty comments about pageants, I just ignored them.

"Like what?"

"Like, they give you poise. They make you confident."

"Why? Because everyone claps and cheers when you smile?"

"You have to answer questions. It's hard, speaking in public, with everyone watching."

The interviews are one of my favorite parts of pageants. I like coming up with good answers. I always wish I could be the one asking the questions, though.

"You can do that in school. Or playing sports," the boy said. He sucked hard on his straw, not looking at me anymore.

"Do you play sports?" I asked.

"No," he said. He almost sounded mad. I thought we were done talking until he added, "I play chess."

"Oh," I said, getting it now. "You're smart."

"Like there's something *wrong* with being smart?"

I was surprised that he could tell what I thought. "I just meant I get why you don't like pageants."

"Why, because smart people can't be pretty?"

What was the matter with this boy?

"Look," I said. Then I stopped, thinking how to say it. "Usually, there are different boxes for different kinds of kids. Smart kids, jocks, good-looking girls. Good-looking boys are usually jocks, so they don't need a separate box. All the average kids go in another box together."

The boy was staring at me again. "Are you frickin' kidding me?"

"I'm not trying to be mean. That's just how it is. Don't you know that?"

After a long pause, he said, "Yeah. I do."

"I'm not saying it's good. I'm just saying that's how it is."

The boy leaned toward me. "But don't you get sick of being in a box?"

"Not really."

He laughed. "Yeah, I guess it's easy being in the good-looking-girl box."

One of the things Miss Denise always says about pageant interviews is not to let your real feelings show. Smile with your words, she says. Smile, smile, smile.

"Not easy, but nice," I said. Smiling.

"Couldn't you be in the smart box, too?" he asked. "You seem pretty smart to me."

It was a good thing I didn't have a piece of fudge in my mouth, because if I did, it would have fallen on the floor. No one had ever said I seemed smart. No one. Ever. Not one time.

"Probably not," I said.

"I've been in a lot of chess tournaments. You're just as smart as lots of the girls there. Maybe not all of them," he said.

"You look pretty young to be in chess tournaments. How long have you been doing them?"

"Eight years. Since I was seven." He sucked on his milk shake, making a gargly, bottom-of-the-glass sound.

Fifteen. He was *fifteen.* He looked as though he would only come up to my shoulder. His face was smooth and hairless and just a little chubby, the way boys' faces are in fourth grade, before everyone starts getting tall. His voice was kind of high.

I thought, *Oh, my Lord,* and then, *A tenth-grader thinks I'm smart.*

"I didn't know seven-year-olds could play chess," I said, struggling to cover up my surprise.

"That's what all the smart kids were doing while you were smiling and waving, I guess."

I remembered Miss Denise and realized I was late. I slid off the stool.

"It was nice talking to you," I said. "I'm Liv Tatum, by the way."

"I'm Danny Jacobson."

"Nice to meet you," I said, feeling suddenly shy. "Maybe I'll see you around."

I'd forgotten about the duffel bag.

"Nah," Danny said. "I just have to pay for this. Then I'm catching a bus."

I wanted to thank him for saying I was smart, but I didn't know how. I didn't have enough money to pay for his milk shake, but I would have if I'd had any extra change. Something about his being short made it seem okay for me to want to do this.

"I hope you win your next tournament," I said, setting my money next to my plate.

"I hope you win, too," Danny said.

three

MISS Denise lives on a cul-de-sac off Mound Street, in a little white house with a gray roof and a fenced-in covered cement porch. Sometimes I have to wait on the porch if she has someone in the kitchen getting her hair cut, which is her real job. But today, when I knocked, she opened the door almost right away and said, “Come on in, Olivia,” like this was a social call and not something my mama was paying her for.

The front door opens onto the living room, which has paneled walls and worn beige carpeting. Miss Denise stood next to her maroon La-Z-Boy while I set down my backpack and pulled off my hoodie. She had her arms crossed, but that doesn’t always mean she’s mad. It’s just how she stands, watching even when she doesn’t have to. It’s like she can’t help it, like she’s so used to analyzing every single move you make that she can’t turn off the judging part of herself.

When I’d dropped my hoodie onto my backpack, she said, “Well, come on now,” and lowered herself into the recliner.

Miss Denise is in her thirties, with dark bobbed hair and long fingernails painted cherry red. It's hard to believe she was in pageants when she was a girl, but she has trophies on the little shelf next to the wood stove to prove it: Diablo County Fair Queen, Arkansas's Ultimate Little Miss, Rock City Firemen's Festival Princess. Now she's thick in the middle and her skin is blotchy, but she still knows what she's talking about. She charges $250 for ten hours of coaching, and if you pay her more money, she'll go with you to the pageant. Mama was working on saving up for that. She had a couple of mule deer in the freezer at Grandma's.

"Let's see you walk, Olivia," Miss Denise said, crossing her legs delicately at the ankles. She wore neon green mules with tufts of green feathers across the tops. Her toenails were painted the same red as her fingernails. "Come on now. Like it's showtime for real."

I stood across the room from her and willed myself to concentrate. Walking isn't just walking, Miss Denise always says. Walking is also thinking about walking.

When I was ready, I began to make my way toward Miss Denise. Keeping track of everything in my head: where my eyes were looking, whether my hands were flat at my sides, whether I was smiling. When I'd walked about halfway across the living room, I did my turn.

Smiling over one shoulder, then the other. Just like I'd done in front of Mama. Just like I'd done a million times. Then I posed long enough for the judges to look at me. *Don't rush,* I told myself. Like Miss Denise always says, the whole point is for them to look.

When I was finished, Miss Denise said, "Where were your eyes?"

"On the TV." Miss Denise has a big plasma TV in the corner. That's where you're supposed to focus.

"No, they weren't. They were looking down."

"I was looking at the TV! At the buttons!"

"Olivia, you were looking at the ground. Now, where are the judges gonna be? Down on the floor or up here?" Miss Denise put on her pageant face: big, hard smile, eyes upturned.

"But—"

"Do it again, Olivia."

I sighed. I knew there would be something wrong every time I did it.

After the next time, Miss Denise said, "Do you need glasses?"

"No. Why?"

"Because you're squinting." She made a terrible face, with eyes all crinkled into lines.

"I didn't do that," I said.

"Well, now, yes, you did, Olivia, and what am I always telling you about talking back?"

I sighed. "That part of being a winner is agreeing."

"Not *agreeing. Being agreeable.* And not arguing." Miss Denise reached for her dental floss, which she keeps on the table next to her recliner, and unrolled a length of thread. She's obsessed with flossing. "No one likes a little know-it-all," she said, angling the floss up between her two front teeth.

I wondered if she knew what she looked like, doing that.

I waited while she flossed. Finally she said, "Let's see you do it again." She was hard to understand, talking with her mouth wide open, working the floss between two back teeth, but I was used to her and knew what she meant.

I walked again. This time it was the way my shoulders weren't even. The next time my smile was too big. "You look like a jack-o'-lantern," Miss Denise said.

"You said to smile!"

"Natural! You want to look natural!"

"But what if I naturally don't smile the right way?"

Miss Denise crossed her arms. This time she was mad. She gave me a look.

"I know, I know. Quit arguing," I said.

She dropped her floss into a little metal wastebasket

next to her recliner. "Let's take a break from all this walking," she said. "Let's do a little singing."

My heart sank. "No. I'll walk some more."

"Now come on, Olivia. Let's hear it."

"Can't I wait until next week? I'm still working on it."

But she was already reaching for her portable CD player. Miss Denise assigns songs to all her pageant girls. Then she buys CDs of the songs, only without the singing, so there's musical accompaniment.

I heard the familiar opening, the old-fashioned piano notes. Keeping my eyes on the plasma TV screen, I started to sing.

Oh! You beautiful doll,
You great big beautiful doll!
Let me put my arms about you,
I could never live without you.

Oh! You beautiful doll,
You great big beautiful doll!
If you ever leave me how my heart will ache,
I want to hug you but I fear you'd break.

Oh, oh, oh, oh,
Oh, you beautiful doll!

Miss Denise switched off the CD player. She closed her eyes.

"Lord, child," was all she said.

"I told you I was still working on it," I said.

I was surprised when she said, "Why don't you sit on the couch for a second? I'm going to get us some 7-Ups."

I never got 7-Up at home, unless I was throwing up.

While she was in the kitchen, I took a look around the familiar living room. It looked different from where I was sitting. The seat part of the La-Z-Boy was old and frayed, the maroon worn to almost gray. The little wastebasket was full of used floss, tangled together like a nest.

Miss Denise came back and set one of two pink plastic cups of 7-Up on the TV tray next to the couch. "Don't worry," she said. "It's diet."

I brought the cup up to my lips and smiled at the tickle of popping bubbles against the bottom of my nose.

Miss Denise took a long sip and set her cup on the table next to the floss.

"Olivia," she said, "I got you in for a lesson with Mrs. Elsie Drucker. Next Monday. I told her you were preparing a song for Prettiest Doll, and she graciously made time in her busy schedule. I told her you were a hard worker. I told her you needed help."

"Monday!"

"Well, the pageant is only three weeks away, Olivia! You've got to get a move on. You're running out of time."

"But I'm not ready for her. I still need to practice. I can do better if I practice on my own first."

The idea of singing in front of Mrs. Drucker made me nauseous.

"You been practicing on your own for months, Olivia. And I got to tell you: it's not helping. And your mama's not helping. Even *I'm* not helping." She looked at me, eyes serious. "Mrs. Drucker's your last chance if you don't want to get up there and make a gol-darned fool out of yourself."

I could feel my face going red. "I'm trying," I said. "I'm trying as hard as I can."

Which wasn't exactly true. I'd sort of given up trying.

"Well, then trying's not helping, either," Miss Denise said. "You need Mrs. Drucker."

"But I've heard stories," I said. "The other girls say she's mean."

Backstage at Little Miss Missouri Starburst, Amber Dickerson said Mrs. Drucker called you names and smelled like B.O.

"What kind of names?" I asked.

"A stuck pig," Amber said. "She says that if you're singing it *right*."

"What's she say if you're singing it wrong?"

Amber flashed her biggest beauty pageant smile at me. "I don't know," she said. "I always sing it right."

"It's not B.O., exactly," Candace Hebert said. She lives in Durham, which is all the way across the state. She's another one I've done pageants with for years. She was born with a cleft palate. After it was surgically corrected, her parents kept entering her in pageants so she would know they thought she was beautiful, no matter what anyone else said. Candace says she doesn't care that she's never won.

"Well, what is it, then?" I asked.

"It's old-lady smell," Candace said.

"Yeah, when the old lady hasn't taken a bath in a week," Amber said.

Candace waited until Amber's name was called for her interview before she whispered to me, "It's not like that at all. Amber is such a bitch."

I nodded. On the other side of the curtain, I could hear Amber saying how her favorite pet was her canary.

"It's like maybe she hasn't taken a bath in *three days*," Candace whispered.

Now I said to Miss Denise, "Why can't I just

dance? I'm pretty good at dance. I don't see why I have to do something I suck at."

"Olivia," Miss Denise said, "I will not have that kind of language in this house."

"Am bad at, then." I always forget how Miss Denise thinks *suck* is foul language.

"Honey." Miss Denise sat forward, like what she was going to say was a truth I had to hear. "You don't do tap. You don't do ballet. That's what the judges want to see from the girls your age. You're still doing what the six-year-olds do: shaking your hips, sashaying across the stage, a cartwheel or two. You do it *better* than they do. But it's the same old thing. And frankly, the judges are tired of it. They want to be wowed."

We don't have tap or ballet studios in Luthers Bridge. The closest ones are in Joplin, which is too far to get to after school, with Mama working. Everything I knew how to do, I'd taught myself from videos Miss Denise had let me borrow.

"You got to face the facts, Olivia. Singing's your only option."

I bit back tears. "I know I can't be good enough at singing to win."

"You don't have to be the *best,*" Miss Denise said. "Why, you're so pretty, you don't have to be even second- or third-best. You just got to be able to get through your song without embarrassing yourself, and you'll win the crown."

"If singing's not important, I don't see why I have to do it at all," I said.

"Well, baby, because then it would just be a beauty pageant, and where's the fun in that?" Miss Denise took a last sip of pop. "Now come on. Let's work on your twirl a little. We're almost out of time."

For the next ten minutes, I concentrated hard on my walk, with the twirl at the end, so the judges could get another good look. Miss Denise nodded the whole time, sliding floss deep between her back molars. "Work it, girl!" she said, her mouth wide open.

At the door, she held up my backpack so I could slide the straps onto my shoulders.

"Good Lord, honey, what are you lugging around in here?" she asked.

"Books."

"Well, for heaven's sake. What are you reading that's so heavy?"

"*First Facts About U.S. History. Math Trek.* A bunch of notebooks."

Miss Denise laughed. "Can't you leave them in your locker?"

"I need them for homework."

"Well, it's terrible for your posture."

"It's okay," I said. "I'm so used to standing straight that I do it anyway."

"But all those other girls without training." She opened the front door. "We're going to be a nation of hunchbacks. Mark my words."

I laughed a little, thinking of teenagers walking around with old-lady humps, how we'd all look crippled and it would be from reading.

Miss Denise frowned. "Good posture's nothing to laugh at," she said, drawing herself up tall to be an example. "Those gol-darned teachers think they know so much."

I stepped out onto the front porch. It felt good to breathe outdoor air.

"Tell those teachers about good posture," Miss Denise said. "Tell them you don't learn everything in school."

I walked down Mound Street, finishing the peanut butter fudge, trying to be happy to be done with Miss Denise for the day, to have nothing to do until bedtime except for a few algebra problems and a vocabulary sheet for French. But I couldn't stop thinking about Mrs. Drucker, how I was going to have to sing in front of her, how unprepared I was. I couldn't shake the feeling of doom.

Mound Street runs all the way through town, from the Kickapoo burial grounds on the north side to the bus station on the south, but there are only businesses on three blocks of it. From the rise at the intersection of Mound and Elm, I could see Mr. White leaving White's Shoes and Mrs. Hayes sweeping the sidewalk in front of the bookstore. Mr. Hutchins was taking in the flag in front of the American Legion post. Mr. White was swatting at mosquitoes on the way to his car.

All the stores on the east side of Mound are redbrick with green awnings, and all the stores on the west side are wood painted all different colors—white and gray and yellow and brown—with no awnings. You don't notice when you're walking from store to store, but up on the hill it's pretty obvious how mismatched everything is. I don't think there was any reason for it; it was just the way the buildings had been built back in the nineteenth century, no one paying any attention to what anyone else was doing, not caring whether anything matched. I kind of like it like that.

I walked slowly down the awninged side of the street, where it was cooler, past Miller's Pharmacy and the Buried Treasure Thrift Shop and Nine Lives Pets and Feed, where I go with Imogene to buy fly spray and wormer and Vita-Hoof. Mrs. Hayes stopped sweeping when I passed and said hi and sorry about all the dust. Her son Cameron is in my grade and does barrel racing, which Mrs. Hayes hates because it's dangerous. "I wish he liked to *read* about barrel racing," she always says, as a joke.

I kept walking, past the Dollar General and Creech's. I crossed Church Street, which is where all the churches are. New Faith Gospel was being painted, so there was scaffolding up. Mr. Jeffries and his son Carson were cleaning brushes at the spigot by the front steps. Carson looked hot in his heavy, paint-stained overalls. He's twenty, and when he was in high school, he was a state wrestling champ. Everyone thought he'd go to Mizzou on a scholarship, but he didn't get enough money. Now he says he's glad he didn't go. He says he likes painting, the way you get to see the whole town from high up.

I stood on the corner, looking past New Faith Gospel, trying to catch a glimpse of Mrs. Drucker's house. It's the nicest house in Luthers Bridge: three stories, made of red brick, with a fan-cooled front porch and square brick pillars and a low, flat-topped stone wall perfect for sitting on during the Fourth of July parade, except that Mrs. Drucker doesn't like kids on her property and chases them off with a broom, not even caring that the whole town sees. There are two big slippery elms, one on either side of the porch, which is ten steps above the sidewalk. The house was built by Mrs. Drucker's husband's grandfather when he owned the only bank in town. Everyone thinks it's a little unfair that Mrs. Drucker gets to live in the house, since she'd only been married to Mr. Drucker for a year before he died of a heart condition. That was forty years ago, but people in Luthers Bridge don't forget. They know Mrs. Drucker was really a Crabtree from Kirbyville and wonder why she didn't just go back there and give someone else a chance to live in the Drucker house.

I thought about how on Monday I was going to have to climb those ten steps and ring the doorbell and wait for Mrs. Drucker to open the glass-fronted door with the pleated chiffon curtain. I was going to have to say "Yes, ma'am" and "No, ma'am" because Mrs. Drucker has a thing about children being rude. I was going to have to pretend that I didn't notice the funny smell. I was going to have to sing.

It was still hot, but I felt a shiver, a quiet knowing that I needed to be rescued, and that, so far as I could see, there was no one around to save me.

four

THE next morning was chilly, as if the recent heat was a dream, or something I'd made up. I didn't want to get out of bed; when I finally did, the floor under my bare feet shot coldness up into my bones. I peeked outside while I was pulling on my jeans. No frost, but everything looked bare and gray. The street was wet, which meant it had rained in the night. It was funny that I hadn't known. Usually, the sound of raindrops on the metal awning over my window wakes me up.

My room is painted pink except for one wall of white bookshelves, but there are only a few books on them. Mostly they're crammed with trophies and crowns from all the pageants I've won or placed in. Some of the trophies are so big that they have to sit on the floor. At night I can just make them out: Little Miss Queen of Hearts, Little Midwest Princess, Ozark Mountain Doll, Glitz 'n Glamour Girl 2004, Adorable Missouri Miss, Lawrence County Sweetheart. I can't even remember all of the pageants I've won them for. A lot of the crowns are from when I was little and don't even fit me now.

I stumbled into the kitchen, where Mama was sitting at the table, sewing sequins onto my Talent dress.

"I thought there were enough sequins," I said.

"A few more can't hurt," she said. "Get a doughnut."

Breakfast is usually day-old doughnuts from Creech's. I pulled a cruller out of the bag and poured a glass of chocolate milk.

"How long you been doing that?" I asked, sliding into my chair.

"Since five."

"You tired?"

Mama looked up. "I should be asking *you* that."

I broke the cruller in two and dunked one of the crescents into my milk.

"Now, Olivia Jane, you gonna come right home this afternoon?"

"It's Friday. I thought I'd go to the barn with Imogene."

Mama put the needle in her mouth and peered fiercely at the sequin she was working on. She held the dress up to the window to see better how sparkly it was. When she started sewing again, she said, "Well, I want you to think about that."

"I have thought about it. I have all weekend to practice."

"Prettiest Doll is coming up. And you got Mrs. Drucker on Monday."

"I know," I said, my heart sinking.

"But I ain't gonna make you. It's up to you. You're a big girl." Mama looked over her reading glasses at me. Then she looked back down at her work. "Up to you," she said.

It was so much worse than if she just forced me. The way she'd been squinting at sequins since before dawn. The way we were eating stale crullers, so there'd be more money for costumes and lessons and the motel in Jefferson City.

"All right," I said. It came out furious, like I'd cursed. I was afraid she'd say I was being disrespectful.

But she just nodded. "I think that's a good decision on your part, Olivia Jane," she said. "I think you're being very mature."

After a minute, she asked, "So are you?"

"Am I what?"

"Tired?" She smiled, like it was a joke.

I didn't answer. I figured she could tell just by looking at me.

I walked fast along Prescott, keeping my head down against the cold, past the Dotsons' house and the Slaters' and Mrs. Springer's and the Guthries'. At the corner, I waited for Cyrus Holley to make a right turn in his beat-up Chevy truck. The bed was full of hay. My eyes watered from the cold.

Dale Hickey Junior High is at the southern end of Mound Street right before the bus station and the road out to the state highway. Lots of towns have middle schools, but Luthers Bridge still has junior high, which means we're just the seventh and eighth grades. I like it like that. In my opinion, sixth-graders are pesky and immature.

The best thing about eighth grade is Mrs. Fogelson, who teaches American history. She thinks of interesting ways to make history less boring. Fortunately, I have history first period. It really helps get me out of bed.

We were working on a class video. I was one of the news reporters covering the Boston Tea Party. I had to tuck all my hair into a tricornered hat and interview Governor Hutchinson and Samuel Adams. I liked thinking of good questions to ask. Mrs. Fogelson said I was the Katie Couric of eighteenth-century Boston.

Mama always says lots of anchorwomen and weather girls did pageants when they were young.

I found Imogene standing in our usual spot, in front of the gym. She was shivering in her Barnstable

Farm sweatshirt. "I hate this," she said. "I can see my breath."

"I wish we lived somewhere warm," I said. "In Australia, they celebrate Christmas on the beach. Because it's the Southern Hemisphere, so it's summer in December."

"I hate the cold, but it should be cold at Christmas," Imogene said.

Imogene always likes for things to be a certain way.

"I can't go to the barn this afternoon," I said. "I have to go home and practice singing."

"But it's the weekend!"

I was glad she sounded like she would miss me.

"I have Mrs. Drucker on Monday. I *really* have to practice."

"But—"

"No, really. I suck. I suck intensely."

"I'm sure it's not that bad."

"Imogene." I made her look deep into my eyes. "Really. You have no idea."

"Okay, so sing for me. Right now."

"I am not singing here."

"Come on." She pulled at my sleeve, leading me around the side of the gym, where no one else was standing. "You're always saying how bad you are. Let me hear."

"Imogene! No!" I pulled my arm out of her grasp. "Quit making me!"

"Well, how the hell are you going to sing in front of a stranger if you can't even do it in front of me?" she asked.

"It's easier in front of strangers," I said.

Sometimes I try to imagine what it would be like if pageants were held in the Dale Hickey Junior High auditorium, in front of Principal Sweeney and Mrs. Fogelson and all the boys I know. Les Dodge, who made out with Madison Belcher when he was twelve and she was fourteen. Joe DeWitt Jr., whose dad's in jail for cooking meth. Landon Terwilliger, the first boy I ever kissed, who once said all the boys voted me the prettiest, and when I asked who was the smartest, he said they didn't vote on that because who cared.

I'd never be able to walk around in fancy dresses and smile over my shoulder and pose for everyone to get a good look if people I knew were the ones looking. Then it would be like I was showing off.

"I hate you tearing yourself down," Imogene said. "I'm sure you're not as bad as you say."

"I am. It's like you and swimming."

Imogene didn't learn to swim until she was eight, and even now she can't put her head down.

"Oh, my God."

"See? That's what I'm saying!"

The bell rang. Everyone started heading toward their classrooms, looking for once as if it wasn't so bad to be going inside, where at least it was warm.

"What are you going to do?" Imogene asked, right before we had to split up, her to Algebra, me to History.

"I don't know," I said, feeling a little flame of hot happiness deep inside, thinking that for the next forty-five minutes, anyway, I got to interview Revolutionary War heroes and not think about singing.

I was all set to head home after school, but on the way Mama called my cell and told me to meet her at Grandma's. I sighed. Grandma lives over on Gibbs Road, and it was starting to rain.

When I got there, I let myself in with the key Grandma gave me for emergencies. I knew she wouldn't be there: she works at the VA and her shift isn't over until five. As I closed the door, I heard Mama calling from the basement, "Olivia Jane? Is that you?"

"Yes," I said. I pulled off my boots and headed down the steep, shag-carpeted steps.

The basement is where Grandpa did all his taxidermy. There are a couple of heads mounted on the walls: a mule deer and a caribou he bagged decades ago. When I was little, I named them Bert and Ernie.

There are two stainless-steel-topped worktables in the middle of the room, two chest freezers on opposite walls, a smaller table topped with a fleshing machine, a freeze dryer, and shelves full of supplies: sculpting compound, casting resin, Fish Coat, Clear-Tex epoxy, mannequins, plaques, glass and plastic eyes, pieces of driftwood, domes and cases.

It's the eyes that get me. I'm pretty much used to everything except the eyes.

Mama was caping a mule deer. From the basement stairs, where I stood, I could see her using her field dressing knife to cut up the back of the buck's neck and around the antlers. She was concentrating hard under the harsh glare of the gooseneck lamp, looking just the way she'd looked that morning, sewing on sequins.

"Well, what're you standing over there for?" she said, barely glancing up. "Come down here. Dry yourself off with that towel by the sink."

"I'm okay here," I said. There was a weird smell in the basement, even though Mama always used deodorizer. "How come you're not at Creech's?"

"I sweet-talked Jim. Carol-Ann was at Mulgrew's picking up trophies for Jordan's soccer team. Luckily.

She woulda never let me leave. Jim's an old pushover, though." Mama squinted and leaned in close to part the hair at the back of one of the antlers. "I told him I had a lot of work here this weekend. He was real nice about it."

"Why do I have to be here?"

"We gotta practice. I figured we could do it here as easy as at home."

"*I'm* the one who has to practice," I said.

"Well, but how you gonna know you're doing it right if there's no one around to watch you?" She put down her field knife and picked up her X-Acto to cut one of the ears off the head.

I looked away. Ears are like eyes.

"There's plenty of room to walk," Mama said. "Between the tables. Just watch out for the corners. You don't want to get all bruised up."

"I'm not walking down there," I said. Then, because I didn't want to hurt her feelings, I said, "I think I'm allergic to all the fur."

"Well, all right, then. Sing."

I thought of everything I wanted to say: I'm tired. It's the weekend. It's too cold down here. Please don't make me. But the way she sat on the stool, hunched over, her forehead all wrinkled, breathing through her mouth with seriousness and trying-to-get-it-just-right, I didn't want to argue.

"Oh! You beautiful doll,
You great big beautiful doll!
Let me put my arms about you,
I could never live without you."

She set the deer head on the tabletop and pulled her reading glasses off her nose, letting them dangle from the chain around her neck. She let her head bob a little in time with the words.

She smiled when I finished. "Well, now, honey, that was wonderful. Just wonderful! How about one more time? And don't forget to find those judges with your eyes and sing it just for them!"

I knew I was being lied to, knew her nice words were faker than the glass eyes she kept in Grandpa's old Rapala fishing lures box. The anger came on me all of a sudden. It took me over. I was speechless with it. I felt it rising up from down deep, clogging up the back of my throat.

"Oh! You beautiful doll,
You great big beautiful doll!
If you ever leave how my heart will ache,
I want to hug you but I fear you'd break."

I kept my eyes on the far wall the whole time, afraid to look at her, afraid she would see the anger on my face.

When I sang the last line, I swear I saw Ernie blink.

five

IT rained all day Saturday. Mama made me practice twice. She kept smiling and praising. I kept saying I had a stomachache and needed to lie down for it to pass. But it wasn't a stomachache, and it wasn't passing.

Sunday was church. The rain let up, but the sky was gray with thick, low clouds. Mama made pancakes, which is our Sunday tradition. We ate with napkins hanging out of our collars so we wouldn't get syrup on our good clothes.

Like always, we drove to church, even though it's less than a mile away. The roads were muddy from the rain; Mama didn't want to get her cuffs dirty. Also, walking is hard for her, since she's so fat. She gets out of breath and sweaty after one block.

We got there just as everyone was going inside to sit down. Mrs. Carle was playing "O Worship the King," and Pastor Templeton was sitting near the pulpit, reading the Bible, not paying any attention to everyone talking. He's round, with a fringe of gray hair around his bald head. His suit was frayed, with an old-fashioned-looking vest that didn't cover his middle. I wish he wore robes, like Father Moriarty at Saint Perpetua, which is Imogene's church. But Baptist preachers are supposed to look like everyone else.

Mama and I sat next to Trudy Dooley and her mother, Mabel Richter. Mama met Trudy when Trudy's son Raymond and I were in first grade together. Raymond is at Dale Hickey, but he takes different classes, so I never see him at school. And Trudy says he won't go to church anymore; he wants to stay home with Mr. Dooley and work on the Impala. "You're so lucky, Janie," Trudy said to Mama, leaning in close and fanning herself with the bulletin, even though it was cold and damp in the nave, "with a girl."

"Oh, I know. I *know,*" Mama said.

"Boys are nothing but trouble, with their cars and their sports and their crazy friends and their, you know, *changes,*" Trudy whispered, holding Mama's gaze in a meaningful way. I didn't know what changes she was talking about, but something about the way she said it, and knowing it was Raymond she was saying it about, made me a little sick.

"Oh, I know," Mama said. "Girls are *easy.*"

They both looked at me and smiled.

"Not *easy,*" I said. I felt offended. I didn't want to let Mama off the hook.

But they just laughed. Mabel Richter, who was almost deaf, said loudly, "Let's save this for *after* church," because she always assumes that, when people are laughing, they need a scolding. I saw Mama and Trudy sneak glances at each other. Mama put her hand up to her mouth to stifle a giggle. It was nice to see her with a friend. Suddenly I felt my lungs filling with air, the relief of a deep breath.

When it was time for the sermon, Pastor Templeton stood up slowly and waddled to the pulpit. "I was thinking this morning about bad times," he said, which was his way of starting a sermon about being submissive to the Lord.

He droned on for an hour. I barely listened. If a minister wants you to pay attention, he should make an effort not to be so depressing.

When church was over, Mama and Trudy and Mabel Richter made a beeline for the ladies' auxiliary food table: ham and fried chicken and macaroni salad and pickles and ambrosia salad and brownies. Everyone was standing around, shoveling food into their mouths and gossiping. The air was sticky and warm and smelled of everyone's breath mixed with Miracle Whip. Suddenly I wanted to be outside, no matter how cold it was. I took my paper plate and snuck out the side door.

There's a cement stoop at the corner of the building, back where the weeds almost never get mowed, across from the toolshed. I sat down and balanced my plate on my knees. I leaned forward and inhaled the good smell of church food. Mabel Richter is a pain in the ass, but she sure can fry chicken.

I was spooning ambrosia into my mouth when I heard someone whisper, "Hey."

It came from the toolshed. For a split second, I thought about ignoring it, but then I heard it again.

"Who's there?" I asked, making my voice loud. Sometimes we get homeless people who've taken the bus as far as they can. I didn't want anyone thinking I was going to hand over my lunch just because I was scared.

"Danny."

I didn't know any Danny.

"You shouldn't be out here. You shouldn't be talking to me," I said. "Now scat or I'll get the pastor."

The shed door creaked open, and then I saw him and remembered.

"Danny Jacobson? From that store with all the candy?" He looked mussed up and unwashed. There was straw in his uncombed hair. I couldn't remember if he'd looked that way on Thursday.

"Turner's," I said. "What the hell?"

He ran his hand through his hair, trying to comb it with his fingers. Then he brushed off his jeans, as if there was dirt on them. I could see he was embarrassed to be so rumpled.

"What are you doing in there?" I asked, but trying to be gentler this time. I felt bad that he was embarrassed.

"Hey, keep it down," he said. "I slept in there."

"Why? Don't you live somewhere?"

Maybe Danny was homeless. But usually, homeless kids have moms.

"Texas," he said. "Houston."

"What are you doing here?"

He brushed his hair off his forehead, reminding me that he was fifteen, not ten.

"I can't be home right now," he said.

"Why not?"

He looked over my head, toward the front of the church, where the parking lot is. I turned to look, too. A few people were hurrying toward their cars, but not many. Most everybody was still inside, eating.

"I'm really hungry," Danny said. "Can you get me something?"

I eyed him, thinking maybe he was a criminal, running away from the police.

"Just a brownie would be okay," he said.

I stood up and held out my plate. "Take it. I'll go get more."

He grabbed the plate from my hands, picked up a chicken leg, and tore off a bite. He didn't even say thank you, which was how I knew he was starving. Somehow, just looking at him, I could tell he was the kind of boy who said thank you under normal circumstances.

When I came back, he was standing just where I'd left him, the plate almost empty except for the ambrosia.

"Here," I said, getting close enough to put two more chicken legs on the plate.

He smiled. My heart suddenly felt like a big wad of something sticky—bubblegum, taffy—being pulled apart.

"Don't you like ambrosia?" I asked.

"This stuff?"

"Yeah. It's fruit salad. Those red things are cherries."

"I don't really like marshmallows unless they're melted," Danny said.

I sat back down on the cement stoop and started eating. Danny lowered himself cross-legged onto the grass. He took a bite of another chicken leg, not as frantically as last time. There was a mustache of grease on his upper lip.

"So what are you doing here?" I asked again.

He kept his eyes on his chicken leg, still chewing. "At home it's just my mom and me. My mom's all right. She wants everything to be okay for me. I know that."

He swallowed. "But I can't talk to her. She won't listen. It has to be her way."

"I know," I said.

"And the thing is, she knows I don't want to do it. And she doesn't care. She says, 'Do it for me, Danny. Do it for your mother.' And when I say no, she gets mad all over again."

"Do what?" I finally asked.

He was eyeing the ambrosia still on his plate. Carefully, he forked a cube of pineapple into his mouth. He chewed and swallowed.

"I have a deficiency," he said.

"Is that like a disease?"

"Not exactly. I was born with it. I don't make enough growth hormone."

"What's that?"

"A chemical. My body doesn't make enough. It's why I'm so short."

"You're not that short," I said.

I don't know why I lied, except that it seemed like the polite thing to do. Everyone knows that boys are supposed to be tall. It would have seemed mean to agree with him about something so important and so awful.

Danny gave me a look. "You don't have to say that. I know what I am."

"I mean it. I know lots of boys shorter than you."

He shook his head and looked away, and after a few seconds, I said, "Okay. Not lots."

I felt so bad. But he looked relieved.

"She wants me to have shots to make me taller. I'd have to have them every day. For years, maybe."

"Every *day?*"

"And it's expensive. She'd have to work another job to pay for them. She works too hard already, at an assisted living place, being a social worker."

"My mom works two jobs," I said. "It's not so bad. You get used to it."

"She's pretty tired already. Her clients are old and sick and always needing help. She's worn out."

I could tell he was mad. Not at me. Just mad about the whole dang thing.

"Would the shots work?" I finally asked.

"Yeah, they'd work. I'd be taller. So?" He shrugged his shoulders. "They wouldn't make me a better chess player."

"Don't you *want* to be taller?"

He shrugged again. More silence. I fought an urge to fill it up with questions.

"So I ran away," he said. "About a week ago. I left her a note, so she'd know I'd be okay. I told her I would call her when I could."

“You can use my cell,” I said.

“No, because then the police could figure out where I was and come and get me.”

“Really?” I was impressed at how much he knew, how smart he was. “She must be worried.”

At least he’d left his mama a note. But he should have told her why he was leaving. I never did find out why Uncle Bread just up and left. He never said. It was disrespectful, really, after all he’d said about loving me like a daughter.

“I can’t let myself think about that,” Danny said.

“Do you have money for motels and food? Do you know where you’re going?” I asked. There was so much I wanted to know, all of a sudden.

“A little money. I’ve been sleeping on the bus,” he said.

“Where do you take showers?”

“I wash a little in bus station bathrooms.” He looked embarrassed. “I’m probably not very clean.”

“I don’t understand,” I said. “What are you going to *do?*”

There was people noise behind me, and I turned to look. Everyone was filing out of church, bundling into coats against the cold, heading off to their cars. I realized I’d forgotten it was cold.

"I have to go. My mom's going to be looking for me," I said. "But I'll come back later."

"I was going to go out," Danny said. "I've been in this shed since yesterday. The bus doesn't come until tomorrow morning."

"What bus?"

"The one to Chicago."

"Is that where you're going?"

"That's where I bought a ticket to," he said. "But I got off here, just to stretch my legs, and then I went into that store–Turner's, you said?–and that milk shake was so good. I lost track of time. The bus left without me. So I have to wait until Monday for the next one."

"What's in Chicago?"

He paused.

"It just looked like a cool city," he said.

"My school's up Mound Street a few blocks. Dale Hickey Junior High. There's woods behind the basketball courts. I can be there around three," I said. "I could bring more food."

He stood up and handed me his grease-streaked paper plate. "Don't bring any of that ambrosia stuff," he said. He turned and loped back toward the shed. "I gotta hide until they all clear out. Thanks," he whispered, half looking back at me over his shoulder.

I slipped in the back door and threw away the plates. Mrs. Carle was sponging down the countertops in the kitchen. "You been outside this whole time? You'll catch your death," she said. "I think your mama's out front."

Mama was already in the car when I found her. "Well, where you been?" she asked. She was in a good mood from Trudy and all the food.

"I took a walk," I said.

"Are your shoes muddy?" She craned her neck to look down at my feet, her good mood evaporating. " 'Cause you know I don't like mud in my car, Olivia Jane."

"I know," I said.

"You take 'em off on the front steps, just to be sure," she said, pulling away from the curb. "I don't want that mud on my carpets."

I nodded, too tired to say anything, thinking how, all my life, there'd be shoes I'd have to check, mud I'd have to scrape off, carpets I'd have to vacuum. So much effort to be clean and pretty and new-looking. Just thinking about it wore me out.

six

I managed to get out of the house by telling Mama I was going for a jog. "So I'll look toned for Prettiest Doll," I said.

"What do you need a backpack for?" she asked, running a knife around the inside of a cake pan she'd just pulled out of the oven. The kitchen smelled vanilla-y.

"Extra weight. Books," I lied. "Miss Denise says extra weight is good for toning."

"You just watch that mud," she said. "And the puddles."

The sky was still thick with clouds, but every once in a while there was a hole and you could see past all the gray to blue. I love that—the way the blue is always there, even if you can't see it. I kept looking up, heading up Mound Street, forgetting all about the puddles, hoping for a glimpse of blue.

Danny was sitting on a downed shagbark hickory where the basketball courts give way to woods. His hair was wet and slick, with comb marks running through it.

"You look clean," I said.

"I washed up at the gas station," he said. "And I washed some clothes in the sink."

"How are they going to dry?" I asked and then saw behind him how he'd hung them over some low-hanging boughs. Two shirts and two pairs of underwear. I looked back at him.

"I bet you were in Scouts," I said, trying not to let my embarrassment about the underwear show.

"No, I hate that stuff. I just brought Woolite and a hair dryer from home. I used the hair dryer in the bathroom to get most of the water out. They can air-dry till morning."

I sat down on the log and let the backpack slide off my shoulders. "I can't believe you thought of that. The hair dryer, I mean." I pulled the backpack around to my lap. "I probably would have just gone to a laundromat."

"Laundromats cost money."

He said it as if I was acting all superior, as if going to a laundromat was the same thing as going to Buckingham's for barbecue every night of the week.

"It's not like we're rich," I said. "I told you my mom works two jobs."

"What about your dad?"

"He's dead."

"Sorry," he said. He looked as though he really was. "My dad's just an asshole."

"Yeah," I said. I know a lot of kids whose parents are divorced. Some of them like their dads; some of them don't. I just let people say how they feel and don't say what I really think, which is *At least your dad's not dead.*

"You go to all those pageants, though," Danny said. "Those things cost money."

"Hey," I said. "I know that. You think I don't know that? You think my mom works two jobs for fun?"

"Okay, okay. *Sorry.* Jeez."

I hugged the backpack close.

"Now maybe I'm sorry I brought you food," I said. "Maybe you're just going to think, *Oh, this rich girl's showing off how much* food *she has.*"

Actually, I had worried about giving him our food when we had to be so careful about money. I talked myself into it by saying that that's what Jesus would do. But it got on my nerves, the way Danny was acting all judgmental about pageants. It wasn't his business how Mama spent our money.

"No. I won't think that. Really," he said.

He had long eyelashes, which I hadn't noticed before. Sitting this close, I couldn't stop looking. If he were a girl and did pageants, he wouldn't even need false ones.

"Really," he said again, and then looked at me hard and deep, until I felt myself believing him.

"Well, okay," I said.

"So what did you bring?"

I handed over the backpack and he unzipped it fast.

"It's just cold cuts and bread and a couple of stale doughnuts," I said. "One of my mom's jobs is at a bakery and she gets to take the day-old stuff home."

"Chocolate glazed are my favorites," he said, pulling out the plastic grocery bags I'd stuffed almost full. I thought he'd eat one right then, but he zipped the backpack up and held it out to me. "Thanks. This is great. This'll get me through till tomorrow."

I remembered then that he was leaving in the morning. I realized that I'd never said goodbye to someone I'd never see again, except my dad, who didn't really count because when I said goodbye to him I was four. Also, I didn't know he was going to end up dead on the 475.

"Do you know *anybody* in Chicago?" I asked.

"Not really."

"So it's just because you think it looks nice?"

"It'll have snow. I've never seen snow."

"Missouri has snow. You've never seen it, really?"

He shook his head.

"It's not that great," I said. "It's pretty when it first falls and sticks, but then it gets gray and slushy."

"I just want to see it," he said. "Sometimes, you just want something different, even if it isn't better."

"I guess I get that."

"I'm sick of southern accents. And rodeos. I hate the rodeos," he said.

"Wouldn't you want to go somewhere with a beach?"

"I don't know. Not really."

"No one hates the beach," I said. I wasn't sure about that, because I've never actually been to a beach, or at least not a beach with an ocean attached to it. I'd gone to Table Rock Lake with my grandpa once, but we just rented a boat at the marina near Lunker Landing and fished for striper.

"Beaches just aren't my thing," he said.

He did look pasty.

"I think it'd be nice," I said, "sitting on a towel, getting tan, watching the waves. Your skin smelling like coconuts. Maybe it'd be like on TV, where waiters bring you pop in glasses on a tray. Maybe it's not really like that, but that's how I like to think of it." I rubbed my hands up and down my arms, trying to get warm. "Just one time, I'd like to order a Shirley Temple on the beach. And not worry about how it's really just 7-Up and the restaurant is giving it a fancy name so they can charge more."

"It figures you'd like the beach," Danny said.

"Why? 'Cause I want to lie in the sun? 'Cause I want someone to bring me a Shirley Temple for once?"

Danny looked at the ground and dug his toe into the soft, wet dirt. "I've got better things to do than just lie around," he said. "And anyway, all that sun gives you skin cancer."

We sat without talking for a bit. I thought how we had nothing in common. He played chess, like Richard Androtti, who smells like benzoyl peroxide and the inside of an old suitcase. And Danny was kind of nasty, the way he made comments about how I looked. I was used to it—people always think that if you do pageants and are pretty, you must be a jerk or stupid—but I usually stay away from people who think things like that.

Still, I didn't like the idea of never seeing him again.

"I know someone in Chicago," I said. "You could stay with him. He wouldn't mind. He loves helping kids."

"That's okay," he said. "I'm used to being on my own." He grabbed a dead hickory leaf and rolled the stem between two fingers. "Who do you know?"

"Uncle Bread."

"Uncle who?"

"It's Fred, really, but when I was little I called him Uncle Bread and he liked it so much I kept doing it. He lives in Chicago. In an apartment. On the third floor."

"I don't know," Danny said. "I don't even know him."

"He's a teacher. He teaches fourth grade. He cares about kids. Really cares about them. Even the ones the other teachers don't pay attention to, who read indoors at recess, or have only one friend, or maybe none. The ones who would rather play video games than basketball. The ones who don't stand out enough and get ignored or left behind. All of them. He would really like you," I added.

"I wish I had a teacher like that."

"The kids love him. Everybody loves Uncle Bread," I said proudly. "Except Mama. Uncle Bread doesn't believe in pageants, which gets her all riled up. And she doesn't like that he moved to Chicago to teach poor kids in the ghetto when there are plenty of Missouri kids who need help. And also, she's not crazy about his being gay. She says there are classes he could go to, pastors who could pray it right out of him."

Danny laughed. "Don't tell that to *my* gay uncle. He's a lieutenant in the Houston Fire Department. Nobody messes with *him*."

I felt a flare of jealousy that Danny's uncle lived in the same city with him.

"Wouldn't your uncle ask me about my parents?" Danny asked. "He would probably call the police if he knew I'd run away."

"No, he wouldn't. Not if I told him not to," I said.

Actually, I wasn't sure about this.

"I don't know, Liv. I think teachers have to tell. I can't take the chance that he'd report me. I'd have to go back," he said.

I felt a shiver, hearing him say my name.

"You don't have to say you ran away. You can say you're seventeen and a high school graduate. Seventeen's only two years older than fifteen."

"He's not going to believe I'm seventeen. He's not going to believe I'm fifteen," Danny said.

"Maybe he would," I said.

Danny pulled something crumpled from his jacket pocket and smoothed it out against the hickory log. It was a bus schedule. I watched him study it. I wondered if the lines in his forehead really did make him look taller, or if that was just me wishing.

"The bus to Chicago leaves tomorrow at six forty a.m.," he said. "It gets to Chicago at seven fourteen p.m." He was quiet for a while, thinking. "Would your uncle mind if I got there at night?"

"He wouldn't like you walking around," I said. "He'd want to meet you at the station."

"What's his last name? I'm not calling him Bread."

"Tatum, same as me. Fred Tatum. You can call him Fred."

"Mr. Tatum," Danny said. He stuffed the bus

schedule back in his jacket pocket. Then he sat, a little hunched over, his hands dangling above the leaf-covered mud. "It would be nice to have a place to stay until, well, until . . ."

"His apartment's really nice," I said. "I've never been there, but he sent me pictures. His front window looks out over the street, and there's a tree that grows up from the sidewalk, and in the spring he can see the new green leaves up close. And there are two fireplaces: one in the living room and one in the bedroom. They don't work, so he put stuffed gorillas in them. He has a thing about gorillas."

"I didn't say I was definitely going," Danny said. "That's kind of weird, a grown man who collects stuffed animals."

"What's weird about it?" I asked, even though I knew. "Don't say he's weird." I was afraid I might cry. "Don't *ever* say a mean thing about him."

"Sorry." Danny looked over at me and then back down at the ground. The dead hickory leaves looked like shattered pieces of frosted glass. "I'm sorry."

"He's my daddy's brother. Was." I blinked hard. "He's all of my daddy I got left."

Danny didn't say anything more, but I could tell he was thinking *Sorry* again and meaning it.

"After my daddy died, Uncle Bread wrote me a

letter a day. He knew I liked getting mail. I kept every one of those letters," I said.

"Wow."

"A hundred and twenty-three, I think. I sent him drawings and then some letters, after I learned to write. He stopped writing after a while. But I keep every one of those letters in my treasure box, tied with a blue ribbon."

He stopped writing when I stopped writing back. I didn't feel like telling Danny that it was too hard, that I was too angry.

"I never get letters," Danny said. "I get e-mails. But letters would be nice."

I was quiet. My anger about Danny saying Uncle Bread was weird was getting all mixed up with the anger about Uncle Bread leaving Luthers Bridge. I tried to sort it all out until it just got too complicated and I stopped.

"It must be hard not having a computer," I said finally.

"I miss virtual chess," he said. "And YouTube."

"The thing is," I said, and then stopped. Mama always says I'm a worrywart and not to borrow trouble. But I couldn't help it. "Let's say you get to Chicago, and you don't call him. Then what?"

"I haven't thought that far ahead."

"I don't believe you." That was when I realized he was going to Chicago for a reason that he wasn't telling.

When he didn't say anything, I said, "Playing chess is all about thinking ahead, isn't it?"

"Okay, so I've *thought* about it. I just haven't decided yet. But I'll figure it out."

"You won't have a computer or a phone." I didn't say that people would notice him, thinking he was a little kid cutting school.

He sat up straight to look at me. "I've been doing all right so far, haven't I?"

"Don't be mad." Almost without thinking, I reached out and let my hand rest on his arm. I felt it then: all my insides rearranging themselves, making room for this new thing.

In your head, you think it's going to be a kiss on a beach at sunset, the sky lit in red and purple streaks. Or maybe in a fancy restaurant and he reaches across the table to grab your hands, and the candles throw up a flickering light so you can see his eyes are wet.

You don't think it's going to be on the basketball courts at Dale Hickey Junior High, with his underwear flapping in the breeze behind you.

“I’m not mad,” he said.

My phone rang just then, making it so we had to look away from each other. When I answered, Mama said, “You been running all this time, Olivia Jane?”

“Yeah,” I said. “Pretty much.”

Anger, shoving at me from the inside, pooling under my skin.

“You don’t sound very out of breath,” she said.

“I’m taking a break,” I said. “Those weights are heavy.”

Danny and I looked at each other, and he smiled, like it was both of us lying instead of just me.

“Where are you, honey?” Mama asked.

“Near the school.”

“You want me to drive over and pick you up? Sky looks awful dark.”

“It’s okay. I’ll be back in a few minutes.”

“Well, all right. You remember what I said about muddy shoes?”

“I *remember.*”

“I don’t like that, Olivia Jane.”

“Sorry.” I rolled my eyes at Danny, not wanting him to think that I was *really* sorry, willing him to forget that thirteen is two years younger than fifteen. “I’ll be right there.” I snapped my phone closed. Looking up, I saw that Mama was right: the clouds were low and looked full to bursting. A wind rustled through the woods around us. The trees shook themselves, whispering *Hurry*.

"You got a pen?" I asked.

Danny fumbled in his jacket pocket. When he handed me a pen, I grabbed the bus schedule and started writing in one corner.

"This is Uncle Bread's number, just in case you do end up in Chicago. Tell him you're my friend. And this is my cell phone number, so you can call me when you get to wherever you end up. Just so I know. I won't tell anyone. I promise."

He stared at the number. "I know."

I stood up. "I've got to get back."

He nodded. "I'm going to stay here awhile. Just until my jeans dry a little."

"Good luck," I said. "If you do decide to call Uncle Bread, he'll take good care of you. Even if you don't need taking care of," I added, knowing he would want to start an argument.

When I turned toward the schoolyard, I felt the first drops. I wanted to ask him wouldn't his jeans just get wet all over again in the rain, but I knew if I did that, he would know that I didn't want to leave—didn't want him to leave—so I forced myself to be still and just start running.

seven

IT rained all night. I know because I didn't sleep. I lay in bed listening to the sound of the drops on the metal awning, wondering if Danny had gone back to the church shed or if he'd just stuck it out in the woods behind the school, thinking maybe the trees would keep him dry. I figured he'd gone back to the church: maybe he'd left things, assuming he'd sleep there. Also, it would be risky to camp out in the woods so close to a school, where kids showing up in the morning might wonder who he was and report him.

I wondered about a lot of things, lying there. I thought about Luthers Bridge, the ramshackle, mismatched shops on Mound Street, church bells ringing on Sundays. Sweet corn in summer, prairie king snakes smelling of musk, sliding through the downed fall leaves, the first snow glittering on the patchy lawns. Mrs. Hayes keeping her stretch of sidewalk clean. Mrs. Fogelson. Imogene at the barn, nudging Honey with her knees, neither of them minding the flies and the dust. Mama. It was everything I knew, the whole world, except for the world out past the hills, where Danny was heading. Danny, who thought I was smart.

And Uncle Bread, in Chicago.

The anger came and went.

Some people never get farther than where they start from, never find out what else there is, or ask questions, or get answers. Cal Burney, who works behind the counter at Nine Lives Pets and Feed, told Imogene and me he'd never been anywhere he couldn't ride his horse to. Don't you ever think about Paris? Imogene asked, or Rome? And Cal said no, he never did.

It was one way to live, I guessed, as I lay there trying to stop myself from shaking.

I got up at 5:30, just as the darkness started to fold over on itself into the gray, damp morning. I tiptoed around so Mama wouldn't know I was up, getting ready. I left the note I'd written the night before on the kitchen counter, near her purse.

Dear Mama,

When you get this, I'll be gone. I'm with a friend, so don't worry. Not Imogene. Someone you don't know but you would like. I'll call you when I can. Don't worry. I know you will anyway. But don't.

I am a terrible singer and I always will be. Lessons won't help.

I'm through with pageants for good.

Don't worry.

Love,

Liv

I closed the front door as quietly as I could. Everything was soaked with the night's rain. The air smelled like wet dirt. I walked until I was in front of the Dotsons'. Figuring I was out of earshot, I pulled out my phone.

"What?" Imogene's voice was ragged with sleep. "It's still nighttime."

"It's after six." When she didn't answer, I said, "Imogene! Don't fall back asleep! This is important!"

"What?"

"I'm leaving."

I could hear the rustling of her sheets as she sat up.

"What do you mean you're leaving!"

"Shhh. Don't wake up your dad! Now listen," I said. "I'm leaving. I'm taking a bus."

"What bus?"

"You're the only one who knows," I said.

"What bus? Where?"

"I'm not going to say, because if you know, you might tell. And I can't answer my cell if you call. But I'll call you when I can."

"What about school? Liv, you can't just not go to school!"

I thought about first period, how Mrs. Fogelson would ask, "Anyone seen Olivia?" when I hadn't shown up for three days in a row. It seemed hateful not to tell her what I was doing, to explain that it had nothing to do with American History. I wished she could know how it was my favorite class, my favorite subject.

"I'll figure that out later," I said.

"What are you saying? You're thirteen!"

"Imogene, I'll be okay. Trust me."

I hate it when people say "Trust me." It usually means they're lying or up to something and just want to shut you up.

"Really. You've known me almost my whole life. I wouldn't do something stupid."

"What about your mom?"

Imogene's mom had died of some rare disease when we were in first grade. We were friends in kindergarten, but we got even closer after. We knew things the other kids didn't. We both felt it was like God gave us to each other after taking one of our parents away.

"I left her a note. I told her I'd be okay," I said. I could feel my brain shutting down, not wanting to think about Mama alone.

"Is it the singing?" Imogene's voice was starting to rise again. "Because I can't believe you're running away because of singing!"

"Not just that," I said.

I couldn't explain it to her: how I couldn't sing "Beautiful Doll" again, ever, or look over my shoulder and wink, or answer another idiotic question about what my favorite color is and why, or which do I like better, cats or dogs.

And how there were things I had to ask, things I had to find out for myself.

And then there was Danny and everything that went with that.

"Running away isn't going to help. You *know* that."

"Imogene! Shhh!" And when there was silence, I said, "I'm sorry. But I have to."

"But what about me? Who will I eat lunch with? Who'll hang out at the barn with me? Who's supposed to be my best friend now?"

She was panicking. Imogene never thinks about how something is going to affect her unless she's scared or angry.

"I am. I'm your best friend," I said. "You can eat with Jenna and Marlena."

"Great."

I knew she was thinking how Jenna and Marlena are

always talking about shopping and being on diets, and how even though they're our second- and third-best friends, they're boring to eat lunch with every day.

"If I were you, I'd be saying the same thing," I said.

"Well, see?" She sniffed. "But you're doing it anyway, aren't you?"

"I have to."

I looked at my phone. It was quarter after six.

"I have to go," I said. "Don't be mad."

"You call me. You *call* me, do you hear?"

"I hear."

"Because this just sucks, that you're doing this."

After a second I said, "You're my best friend."

"Call me, you bitch."

I smiled. I knew she was making a joke.

"I will. As soon as I can, I will."

"Liv," she said, "you're not being kidnapped, are you? There's no one pointing a gun at you, making you say all this, is there?"

"No," I said. "It's just me."

It was starting to rain again. The clouds looked like growling animals, low and threatening in a burrow.

"I have to go."

"Is it a *boy?*"

"It's not a boy," I said, which felt like the truth and a lie at the same time.

★

The bus was in the station, belching out smoke and fumes when I got there. An old married couple wearing matching blue visors and a guy who looked like he was either a college student or homeless were sitting on the benches in the waiting room. The college student had a backpack. The old married lady had a little pink suitcase on wheels. I wondered where Danny was and thought, *I'm going anyway, whether he goes or not.*

I had to get out.

I went up to the ticket window and shoved my money under the glass. "Can I get a ticket to Chicago?" I asked.

The ticket seller was a man I'd never seen in town, too young to be the father of anyone I knew. He had pimply skin and looked as though he was embarrassed to be wearing a uniform. "One-way or round-trip?" he asked, not looking up from his cash drawer.

"One-way." I didn't know he was going to ask. The words just spilled out of my mouth, like a mistake, but even though I knew I could take them back, I said nothing and waited patiently for my change.

Only when I turned around did I see Danny coming out of the men's restroom, his hair wet and combed.

"What?" he said when he realized it was me.

His forehead was crinkled up with the irritation you

feel when you're surprised and it isn't something like a present or a snow day. But I thought I saw something else, too: a little gladness in his eyes.

"Are you still going to Chicago?" I asked. My heart was beating in my ears, and a voice in my head was keeping time with it, whispering, *Say yes, say yes.*

"Yeah." He hoisted his duffel bag higher on his shoulder. "I'm not sure about calling your uncle. I may just want to be on my own. I really appreciate your help, though," he said. I could tell he thought I was going to be mad, was going to start arguing with him again about not knowing anyone, not having anywhere safe to stay.

"Well, I'm going to Chicago, too," I said.

"What?"

"Not because of you. Because of other reasons."

"What reasons? You don't have any reasons."

"How do you know? You don't know anything about me." The old lady glanced over at me. "I have lots of reasons," I whispered.

"Like what?"

I didn't want to say. It was pushy, asking me like that, not even thinking that maybe it was too personal for me to talk about. "I don't have to tell you anything."

A man in a gray uniform emerged from the bus and pushed open the door to the waiting room. "You folks on the six forty to Chicago?" he asked, not looking at any of us in particular. "Backpacks and luggage gotta go in the back."

We fell in line behind the old couple, who were hunched over but fast. You could tell they liked being first in every line they stood in. The old man turned and looked at us, probably thinking we were brother and sister and wondering where our parents were. "You youngsters have any breakfast?" he asked.

"Yeah, we did," Danny said. "At home."

My heart flipped over when he said "we."

"You like those Honey Clusters? I love those Honey Clusters. It's a cereal," he said.

"Yeah," Danny said. "They're good."

"Not too sweet," the old man said. "Now my grandson, he's a Cap'n Crunch man."

"Cap'n Crunch is good," Danny said.

"He'd eat it for breakfast, lunch, and dinner if my daughter'd let him," the old man said. "I never seen a boy so attached to one food before. It ain't normal."

"Oh, *Ed,*" the old lady said.

The old man looked at her and almost said something but seemed to change his mind. He turned back to us. "He'd eat it without milk. Just dry, right out of the box."

"I used to like Cap'n Crunch," Danny said. "But it's a little too sweet."

I let myself pretend that Danny and I were grown-ups—married and on our honeymoon—and Danny was doing all the talking because he knew I was shy about having to make conversation with strangers. Then it was like he was doing all this talking for me, like he was protecting me in a manly, husbandly way. So all this talk about cereal was almost sexy.

"The sweetness kind of gets to you after a while," Danny said.

The bus driver took my backpack and stowed it in the luggage compartment, which was already half-full of suitcases. I looked up and saw people staring out of the bus window. As if he could read my mind, he said, "We started out in Houston." I thought how going somewhere on a bus is different from going on a plane, which is probably thrilling even if you've done it a hundred times. You get to look down at clouds and the world as it slides away behind you. I couldn't even imagine how that would feel: like magic, or when Pastor Templeton talks about the ecstasy of knowing Jesus. The bus passengers were looking out the window with tired eyes. If they knew Jesus, it wasn't showing on their faces.

Danny and I headed toward the back of the bus, where it was emptier. We had to wait in the aisle while the old couple fussed with overhead storage. "Where'd you put my pills, Doris?" Ed asked, standing in the aisle, not even noticing that we were waiting to get past him. "I gotta take two at ten thirty."

"They're in the toiletries bag," Doris said. She was standing over her seat, trying to ease one shoulder out of her powder blue Windbreaker. "Honestly. Can you help me, please?"

"Pills aren't toiletries, for God's sake. Toiletries are shampoo, toothpaste, mouthwash. For God's sake, Doris."

"Will you pull this, please?" Doris offered him a bony shoulder. *"Honestly."*

Ed shook his head at Danny, trying to rope someone else into the conversation. "Pills are medicine, for God's sake. You don't just throw them in a toiletries bag. Don't you know that?" He pulled Doris's Windbreaker off her arm and winked at Danny, showing him that this is how you talk to women. "Last time I let *you* pack the pills," he added. "Now move over. Let me sit down. My knees are killing me."

We found seats and settled in. Danny tucked a brown paper sack under his seat. Then he looked backwards down the aisle, making sure no one was close enough to hear. "Ed and Doris are like my grandparents before my grandfather died," he said. "Always arguing."

"My grandfather's dead, too." It was nice, finding

oplars and Autumn Blaze maples and crape myr-
y favorite. And then there would be snow.

ey," Danny said, "you're fogging up the window."

ıt up and rubbed at the glass with the arm of my
. Now I could see more clearly the passing high-
igns: to Racine and Neosho and Fort Smith,
ısas; to Diamond and Duenweg; to Carthage and
s City.

went to Kansas City once," I said. "Little Miss
ıble Missouri was in Kansas City."

ıre you kidding? That's what it was *called?*"

thought about saying what I always do: that it's
ı name, it's all about inner beauty, you're not
allowed to wear flippers, which are the fake teeth
pageants make you wear if your adult ones haven't
in yet.

ut I didn't. "Yeah," I said. "I know."

I can't believe you do those things," Danny said.

It was at the Marriott, I think. There was an indoor
ıming pool and a whirlpool, and I wanted to sit in
ıt Mama said we didn't have time. The pageant was
ıe of the rooms off the lobby, and the people at the
t desk stared at all of us in our gowns. I think I
e the blue tulle with the violet sash."

"How old were you?"

"Seven. This one girl at the desk, she was probably

out we had something in common. "But they didn't argue. I don't think they were very happy, though."

"How come?"

"Everything was hard. They were always working. It's hard to be happy when there's so much work. And my grandmother is still working, and she's almost sixty."

"What did they do?"

"Grandma's a nurse." I didn't say anything about Grandpa doing taxidermy. I'm used to not telling. It's a secret I always keep with me, like a locket I never take off.

Danny leaned back. He was so short that he didn't even come up to the headrest.

"I'm going to be a doctor," he said. "A pediatrician. That's a doctor for kids."

"I know that," I said, irritated that he thought I didn't. "Everyone knows that."

"I want to be the kind of doctor kids like. The kind who gives out lollipops and makes jokes and doesn't lie," he said. "The kind who, if he has to do something that hurts, just tells you straight out."

I thought about Dr. Parker at the clinic. He's old and seems tired of kids. Whenever he gets out a tongue depressor, I remind him that I can open my mouth really wide and don't need one. He always nods and says “Can’t hurt to save a little scratch” as he slides the tongue depressor back in the glass jar.

“I guess you want to be a beauty queen or something,” Danny said. “A model. A *spokes*model.”

“I haven’t decided yet.”

I’d thought about it, though. All the things I could picture myself being had something to do with looking pretty. It was what I was good at, what I knew how to do. What good was all that smiling and eye contact if I was just going to be making cakes in a bakery?

I felt the bus engine vroom under our seat. For a second, I thought about Mama, who would be waking up in ten minutes and calling for me to come out for breakfast. It would take her another few minutes to realize I wasn’t there, if she didn’t find the note first. My throat closed up, thinking how she would whisper “Oh, sweet Jesus” as she read it.

The bus rumbled away from the station and out onto Mound. On the ramp up to the interstate, it started to gain speed. I watched as the leafless trees became a gray blur, slipping away. I remembered that people in cars we passed might be looking up at me, so I blinked the terror out of my eyes and made sure no one could see what was in my head.

THE land on either side of t
patchy grass and part weeds the c
dered past landmarks I recognize
Elms Shopping Center, the cra
restaurant that had closed down
seen them all before, on drives wi
in Joplin and Springfield, on the f
to the air and space museum in Tul
unfamiliar. I wondered if places
when you’re leaving them behind.

The smell of cow manure. B
Superstores, Fred’s Radiator, Brans
University of Missouri Southwest
I really paid attention, memorizing
sure I wouldn’t forget.

The distance was thick with t
green all year, some had turned, and
bare. Even in the rainy murk, the ye
were like flames, like danger, in all th
would burn out, leaving the gray, t

out we had something in common. "But they didn't argue. I don't think they were very happy, though."

"How come?"

"Everything was hard. They were always working. It's hard to be happy when there's so much work. And my grandmother is still working, and she's almost sixty."

"What did they do?"

"Grandma's a nurse." I didn't say anything about Grandpa doing taxidermy. I'm used to not telling. It's a secret I always keep with me, like a locket I never take off.

Danny leaned back. He was so short that he didn't even come up to the headrest.

"I'm going to be a doctor," he said. "A pediatrician. That's a doctor for kids."

"I know that," I said, irritated that he thought I didn't. "Everyone knows that."

"I want to be the kind of doctor kids like. The kind who gives out lollipops and makes jokes and doesn't lie," he said. "The kind who, if he has to do something that hurts, just tells you straight out."

I thought about Dr. Parker at the clinic. He's old and seems tired of kids. Whenever he gets out a tongue depressor, I remind him that I can open my mouth really wide and don't need one. He always nods and says "Can't hurt to save a little scratch" as he slides the tongue depressor back in the glass jar.

"I guess you want to be a beauty queen or something," Danny said. "A model. A *spokes*model."

"I haven't decided yet."

I'd thought about it, though. All the things I could picture myself being had something to do with looking pretty. It was what I was good at, what I knew how to do. What good was all that smiling and eye contact if I was just going to be making cakes in a bakery?

I felt the bus engine vroom under our seat. For a second, I thought about Mama, who would be waking up in ten minutes and calling for me to come out for breakfast. It would take her another few minutes to realize I wasn't there, if she didn't find the note first. My throat closed up, thinking how she would whisper "Oh, sweet Jesus" as she read it.

The bus rumbled away from the station and out onto Mound. On the ramp up to the interstate, it started to gain speed. I watched as the leafless trees became a gray blur, slipping away. I remembered that people in cars we passed might be looking up at me, so I blinked the terror out of my eyes and made sure no one could see what was in my head.

eight

THE land on either side of the interstate was part patchy grass and part weeds the color of straw. We thundered past landmarks I recognized: Kum & Go Gas, the Elms Shopping Center, the cracked Café sign for a restaurant that had closed down before I was born. I'd seen them all before, on drives with Mama to pageants in Joplin and Springfield, on the fourth grade field trip to the air and space museum in Tulsa. Today they looked unfamiliar. I wondered if places always look strange when you're leaving them behind.

The smell of cow manure. Billboards for Adult Superstores, Fred's Radiator, Branson Radio 1550 AM, University of Missouri Southwest Center. Flying past, I really paid attention, memorizing everything, making sure I wouldn't forget.

The distance was thick with trees. Some stayed green all year, some had turned, and some were already bare. Even in the rainy murk, the yellow and red leaves were like flames, like danger, in all the green. Soon they would burn out, leaving the gray, twiggy skeletons of tulip poplars and Autumn Blaze maples and crape myrtles, my favorite. And then there would be snow.

"Hey," Danny said, "you're fogging up the window."

I sat up and rubbed at the glass with the arm of my hoodie. Now I could see more clearly the passing highway signs: to Racine and Neosho and Fort Smith, Arkansas; to Diamond and Duenweg; to Carthage and Kansas City.

"I went to Kansas City once," I said. "Little Miss Adorable Missouri was in Kansas City."

"Are you kidding? That's what it was *called?*"

I thought about saying what I always do: that it's just a name, it's all about inner beauty, you're not even allowed to wear flippers, which are the fake teeth some pageants make you wear if your adult ones haven't come in yet.

But I didn't. "Yeah," I said. "I know."

"I can't believe you do those things," Danny said.

"It was at the Marriott, I think. There was an indoor swimming pool and a whirlpool, and I wanted to sit in it, but Mama said we didn't have time. The pageant was in one of the rooms off the lobby, and the people at the front desk stared at all of us in our gowns. I think I wore the blue tulle with the violet sash."

"How old were you?"

"Seven. This one girl at the desk, she was probably

twenty or twenty-one. She couldn't stop staring. She came around the desk and leaned down toward me, her hands on her knees, all smiley. 'She's so *cute!*' she said, still staring. *She*. Looking right *at* me. Like I couldn't hear her. Like I was somebody's beagle.

"She stood up and said it again to Mama. 'She's so *cute!*' Then she said, 'Have you thought about having her ears done?' And Mama said, 'Oh, they been pierced since she was three.' And the girl says, 'No, *done*. Like, pinned back. It's an operation. So they don't stick out so much.' "

Danny sat forward and looked at me. "They don't stick out. Your ears look fine."

"That's what I think." Out of habit, I ran my fingers through my hair, making sure that it puffed in just the right way around both sides of my head. "Mama, she just said something polite, like 'Maybe when she's older.' But really, she would have done it if she could. If we'd had the money."

"Maybe not. Maybe she liked you the way you were."

"She did. She does. But she looks at me differently. Since that day. She *peers* at me when she thinks I'm not noticing. Like she's trying to figure out what I would look like with different ears."

Danny looked away from my face to the landscape

out the window: more hills and trees, not so much flatness. The beginning of something new.

"My mom is always talking about how great it would be to be taller," he said. "How taller people get better jobs. How girls like taller boys. She says there are studies that prove that tall people are more successful."

I felt myself blushing about girls liking taller boys.

"I tell her there are different ways to be successful," Danny said.

"Girls don't care so much about being tall. They care more about being thin," I said.

"Yeah, but they like tall boys. You never see couples where the girl is taller." Now he was blushing. He had let me know that he'd checked.

"Movie star couples, sometimes," I said.

He sighed. "That's what everyone says."

"Well, it's true."

"Okay, so male movie stars don't have to worry about how tall they are."

We both stared out the window, which was streaky with rain. The trees that had been far away were closer now. On the other side of the wet glass, they looked smeared and fuzzy edged, like trees a kindergartner had drawn.

"Especially if they're handsome," I said. "That's what everyone is noticing."

We stopped in Springfield for fifteen minutes. Danny left the bus to use the bathroom in the station. I thought about going with him; I didn't like the idea of using the toilet on the bus, walking past everyone's knowing eyes. But I didn't really have to go, and I thought that maybe he just needed some time to himself. While he was gone, I kept watch for him, willing him to come back before the bus driver revved the engine. I practiced saying, "Excuse me! We have to wait for that boy I was with," in case I needed to. When I saw him heading back toward the bus, I thought *Thank the sweet Lord,* and thought of Mama.

When he got back to our seats, he held out a Snickers bar and a Baby Ruth. "Take one," he said.

"Oh, that's okay." I didn't want him to think I was hungry, which I was. I had forgotten about bringing food and had to be careful with my money. I had only fifteen dollars and sixty-three cents left after buying my ticket.

"No, really. I wanted to get you one, but I didn't know what you like."

Carefully, I reached for the Baby Ruth. "Thanks."

"I like them both," he said, sliding into his seat.

I wondered if it counted as a present if he would have eaten it anyway.

The driver, whose nametag said ELROY, hopped back

up the bus stairs and looked out over the passengers. "We all here?" he asked.

"What should we say if we're not?" Ed called out from his seat. A few people around him laughed.

"You a comedian?" Elroy asked, sliding into the driver's seat. "That's all right. I've had my share of comedians."

Now lots of people were laughing, feeling chummy all of a sudden.

"Keep 'em laughing, buddy," Elroy said. Slowly, he steered us out of the parking lot.

"How much money do you have?" I asked Danny when we were back on the highway. I knew it was rude to ask, but somehow the regular rules are easier to break when you're on a bus and no one you know is around to lecture you. It was kind of thrilling.

"A lot. It's bar mitzvah money."

"Bar what?"

"Bar mitzvah. It's a Jewish ceremony. It marks a boy's entry into manhood. You have to memorize a lot of Hebrew and make a speech. It's a big deal."

"Manhood? Come on."

"Yeah, when you're thirteen."

"Thirteen?"

"It's traditional."

"But you still have to go to school. You can't drive. You can't get a job."

"It doesn't mean you're a man like that. It means you're responsible for following Jewish law."

Luthers Bridge doesn't have any Jews. Some kids say mean things about them. Landon Terwilliger stole a Chunky from Turner's once because he said Merle Turner was trying to jew him. That was after he kissed me during halftime at the Mountaineers' football game at the high school. We were in sixth grade back then, and I hadn't yet figured out what an asshole he was.

"Do you go to church?" I asked. I felt shy in a way I hadn't when I'd asked him how much money he had.

"It's called a synagogue."

"My mama says Jews are smart. She says if I was Jewish, I'd have to get good grades and work in a store after school *and* do pageants."

I was proud to be able to say that Mama admires Jews, but Danny shook his head and said, "That's still being prejudiced. Even if you're saying something nice."

I wanted to explain about Mama: that she means well, that in her mind, saying someone is smart is a huge compliment. But then I thought, *Not as huge as saying someone is pretty. Pretty is bigger.*

"Not all Jews are smart," Danny said.

"Yeah, I guess," I said. I was exhausted from saying the wrong thing, from not recognizing anything out the window. We were passing an exit for Sparkle Brook Road. I pictured a creek deep in the forest, a single shaft of sunlight, ferns and moss, that piney smell. There would be a flat, dry bank. You could spread out a blanket and the water splashing over flat stones would lull you to sleep.

I woke up with a crick in my neck, my head against the window, my mouth open. I'd been drooling. I righted myself and licked my lips, praying that Jesus had been watching over me and hadn't let me snore.

"What time is it?" I asked.

"A little after eleven. Boy, you were out. You missed a lot. Look," Danny said, leaning across me and pointing. "The Mark Twain National Forest."

I looked, turning my head toward the window mainly so I could breathe into my cupped hand and check for bad breath. Outside, oaks, hickories, and shortleaf pine rose up and disappeared in the rainy mist. Usually I love trees, but now I resented the way they cast us in shadow, shutting out the thin, gray light.

"My daddy used to shoot wild turkey in these parts," I said, remembering Mama telling me.

Danny was staring with wonder. "So much forest," he said.

"I wish it would stop raining," I said.

"I don't mind it," he said.

We stayed on the interstate through the woods, emerging after a bit, and drove past exits to Waynesville, St. Robert, and Fort Leonard Wood. We passed a camouflage-colored Jeep driven by a soldier in a khaki uniform and hat. Danny and I both waved when he looked up.

I thought we had left the forest behind for good, but more trees loomed in the near distance, and soon we were winding through them. I slept again.

Hunger woke me up. I kept my eyes closed, trying not to think about fried chicken or Mama's cakes. Trying not to think about Mama's cakes made me think about Mama, how crazy worried she must be. I asked Jesus to fill her with the Holy Spirit, to let her know that everything would be all right, and while he was at it, to let me know it, too.

We pulled into a Burger King in Rolla for a lunch break. "They got any restrooms in this joint?" Ed called out as Elroy put on the brake and pulled open the doors.

All the older passengers laughed, knowing that Ed and Elroy had this thing going, this temporary friendship that was making the trip more fun.

"Hey, why don't you do a little investigating while you're out there?" Elroy said. "Why don't you give us a report?"

"Will do!" Ed said, happy to be the center of attention as he waited for everyone ahead of him to file out of the bus.

I was starving, but to save money I ordered fries and a small Diet Coke. The smell of the fries was like joy in my whole body. At home, we almost never had enough money to eat out.

"Is that all you're getting?" Danny asked when I squeezed into the plastic bench across the two-person table from him. He had ordered two cheeseburgers, onion rings, and a Mountain Dew.

"It's all I want," I said.

"Really? Or are you just always worried about getting fat?"

I shook my head no. "I don't even think about that."

Mama isn't like some of the other pageant moms, making their girls eat salads and cottage cheese. She always says I'm naturally thin, the way she used to be, so I can pretty much eat what I want.

Danny took a bite of his cheeseburger and chewed. He had a pale streak of catsup on his lip. I kept waiting for him to lick it off.

"You never told me why you're doing this," he said.

"I have my reasons."

"I told you why I was doing it," he said. "Fair's fair."

You didn't *really* tell, I thought about saying, but I just ate another fry. I didn't want to make him tell. I wanted him to want to.

I unzipped my purse and pulled out my wallet. I tugged the small picture out from behind my Dale Hickey Junior High School student ID, where I keep it hidden. It would be embarrassing for anyone to know I carry it around.

I passed it across the table. "Don't get grease on it," I said.

He studied it for a moment. "Your face. And your hair. It's so big."

"That's what you have to do. That's the whole point. To look like that."

"How old were you in this picture?"

"Six. It was the first time I won. I was so happy. I mean, I can't even explain how happy I was. How it felt to be that happy. Like I couldn't keep all the happiness in my body. Like I was splitting open with it."

And proud. "You did it!" Mama kept saying as we walked back to the car, and I kept wanting to ask, *Did what?* but she was so excited, she was laughing, maybe for the first time since Daddy died, and I was laughing, too, for the first time since Uncle Bread left.

It had felt so good to think that maybe I had saved us both.

"No offense," Danny said, handing the picture back, "but you don't look real. You look like a doll."

I took the picture from him and slipped it back into my wallet. Then, because it was driving me crazy, I reached over and wiped the catsup off his lip with the pad of my thumb. If it had been a movie, I would have licked it off my thumb, but it wasn't. That would have been gross. I just wiped my thumb on my napkin.

"Yep," I said.

nine

THE afternoon was a blur of rain and traffic and highway signs: to Cuba and Owensville, Sullivan and Potosi, Stanton and St. Clair and Union. The interstate, I thought blearily, was like a copper wire, with little towns strung on it like glass beads.

I thought about how each town had thirteen-year-olds living there, going to school, learning the same Missouri facts: how we are the Show-Me State, how Missouri is the eighth largest state in the country, how the Mississippi and Missouri Rivers join up near St. Louis, which is the fifty-eighth largest city. We all know about Mark Twain and George Washington Carver and Harry Truman. I thought of my teachers harping on the same stories, and it started to make a little bit of sense. They were trying to tie us together with knowing the same facts. They were trying to make Missouri our home. I looked out over the passing fields and felt a squeezing ache of goodbye in my chest.

"What do you miss about Texas?" I asked.

Danny was sitting by the window now; I gave up the window seat after lunch, my way of thanking him for buying me a Hershey's sundae pie.

"There's a common room in our apartment building. Some old men play chess there. They don't mind if I watch."

"Is that all?" I asked when he didn't say anything else.

"The beer-can house. Pecan trees." He smiled. "My friend Benny Mittelman. We're in the same confirmation class. We have exactly the same sense of humor."

"What's the beer-can house?"

"Some guy collects beer cans and hangs them from the trees around his house. It's pretty cool."

"Did you tell Benny you were leaving?"

He nodded. "I didn't say where I was going. But I told him I had to get away. He understood. Well, he sort of understood. He doesn't see why I don't just get the shots."

"That's what I told my best friend, Imogene. Because if I'd told her where, she would have told my mama. I know she would have."

He looked at me, impressed. "There's a lot of stuff you have to figure out if you're going to run away. I told you about not using your phone, right?"

"I already knew that, from TV." It wasn't true, but I

didn't like him focusing on how I was so much younger than he was.

"And you have to have a story, in case someone asks why you're not in school. I tell people I've been staying with my grandmother while both my parents are in Iraq, and now my dad is home and wants me to be with him. Well, I *would* tell people that if they asked. So far, no one has." He looked out the window again, where exit signs were announcing streets in St. Louis. "It's always good to say your parents are fighting in the war. It distracts people. Plus it makes them admire you for being so brave, being strong while they're gone, traveling alone."

"I don't have a story." I thought for a minute. "I'll say I'm an orphan and I'm going to live with my Uncle Bread in Chicago. That my parents died in a car crash on the 475 in Georgia, and I was supposed to go into foster care, but Uncle Bread said he wouldn't hear of any such thing, that I had to be with him."

"You can't say you're an orphan. People want to help orphans. That's a pretty good story, though. How do you even know about foster care?"

"There are some kids at my school."

"I think we should have the same story," he said. "It's too weird that two of us are traveling together and have different stories. You could be my sister."

I felt an electric charge all over, that he was lumping me in with him.

"I don't look like you, though," I said.

"It doesn't matter. I'll just tell people that you're my little sister and I'm supposed to be taking care of you. And that you get carsick on buses. It's good to throw in a few details."

I said okay and got up to use the bathroom, even though I didn't really have to go. When I'd closed the door behind me, I just stood in the tiny, rocking space for a minute or two. I needed to be alone, where no one could see, to feel the happiness of Danny taking care of me.

In St. Louis, we got a new driver, whose name was Len. We switched freeways and headed north. Now everyone was tired and cranky from sitting so long. Ed walked up and down the aisle a couple of times, explaining that his knees were seizing up. "You kids okay? You got someone meeting you in Chicago?" he asked on one of his strolls.

"My uncle. Our uncle," I said. "He just got back from Iraq. He won a lot of medals."

I was proud of myself, but Danny sneakily nudged his elbow into my side.

"I was in the service. Army. Great bunch of guys. Great bunch." Ed looked as though he was tearing up. "What branch of the service was your uncle in?"

I started to panic, but Danny said, "Marines. Second Division," as easily as if he was telling someone where he lived.

"Good man," Ed said, using the seatbacks on either side of the aisle to push himself forward. "You tell him I said so." He leaned down and squinted out the window at the endless fields of brown, papery stalks. "Jeez. Enough already with the corn."

When he was out of earshot, I whispered, "What did you poke me for? You said people love it when someone's been in Iraq."

"It's easy to say too much," Danny said. "Don't say anything if you can get away with saying nothing."

I felt my face getting red from my stupid mistake. Suddenly it seemed as though there was too much to remember, too much I'd surely forget, and then I'd have to live with knowing that I'd blown it for both of us.

"Sorry," I said.

"It's okay," he said, reaching under his seat for the brown paper bag. He sat back up and pulled out a hinged wooden box with alternating light and dark squares. "Come on. Let's play."

"Chess?" He was opening the box. Inside, all the pieces lay in purple velvet indentations shaped like themselves. "I don't know how."

"I'll teach you. Come on. I'm bored."

I caught sight of my reflection in the window. I thought how pretty I looked, even though I'd been sitting on a bus for hours. I hadn't thought about being pretty all day, and that wasn't how it usually was for me. Usually, I thought about it all the time. Either Mama brought it up or kids at school looked at me in a way that I knew meant *they* were thinking about it, which made *me* think about it: a whole big circle I couldn't get out of. I won't lie: sometimes it was nice in a flattering kind of way. I mean, who doesn't like it when other people like the way you look?

But it meant I was always in the pretty-girl box, in a velvet hole shaped just like me.

"Sure," I said.

We played for three hours. I had to work hard to hold the names of the pieces in my head. My favorite was the knight, because of the horse, and also because of the zigzaggy way it moves.

I told Danny I didn't want him letting me win. "I wouldn't do that," he said, and when I said, "Okay," he added, "It only means something if you have to work for it," which made me decide to get serious about memorizing the names of all the pieces and the directions you could move them. Which probably didn't matter that much anyway: Danny said the main thing is strategy.

I had no chance of winning, but I put Danny in check once. "Whoa," he said, half-laughing. He saved his king easily and beat me in another three moves, but I could tell he was impressed. "You should do this for real. Join a club or something. Does your school have a chess club?"

"I don't think so," I said. "Dale Hickey is more about football and basketball and cheerleading."

"Not everybody's into sports. What do the kids who don't like sports do?"

"I think there's a Star Wars club," I said. I didn't tell Danny that I had never thought about asking.

"Wait, let me guess. Star Wars—that's the one you're in," Danny said. He was looking down, tucking each pawn into its purple softness. I couldn't tell if he was joking in a mean way or just kidding.

"I'm not in any clubs. I don't have time," I said.

He nodded without looking up.

I wished I could think of something more to say, to mask his disappointment, which was fogging up the silence.

Suddenly, the cornfields were gone, mowed down by flat, crowded towns: Bloomington and Joliet, Bolingbrook and Burr Ridge. Our bus slowed, caught in thick, clogged-up traffic. "It's always the same big ugly mess," Len said loudly, for everyone's benefit. I felt urpy with all the stopping and going.

"It's okay," Danny said. He touched my hand for a split second before taking his away. "We're almost there, I bet."

I nodded, my head too heavy to lift off the seatback. It was dark now, and the car headlights on the other side of the freeway streamed toward us, a lit-up river. In the distance, I could just see the skyscrapers—like nothing I'd ever seen in Luthers Bridge—or in Kansas City, even. And then it was hard to tell whether the skip in my heartbeat was because we were almost there, or because he had known I was queasy without my even saying.

In the station, we waited for Len to throw our baggage out of the cargo hold. Ed and Doris were standing near us, talking quietly just to each other. Ed's eyes had saggy, tired bags underneath them. Doris was wearing her Windbreaker across her shoulders like a cape.

Something about them was different from the way it had been this morning: Doris was the one watching for their bags, thanking Len for putting them in the cart she'd somehow gotten hold of. Ed shuffled stiffly beside her as they made their way out to the street. He was tired; he needed her to do everything.

"You kids all right?" Len asked as he handed me my backpack. "You got someone coming for you?"

"Yeah, thanks," Danny said, slinging his duffel bag

over one shoulder. To me, he said, "Come on, Molly. Up that escalator, I think."

He'd called me Molly so, if anyone reported me missing, Len wouldn't make the connection. I wondered if there was an actual Molly, someone he knew in his real life, or if he just liked the name. "Good strategy," I said when we were out of earshot, making him smile.

The bus station was huge and brightly lit and full of people, so different from the shabby, almost empty platform in Luthers Bridge. Men and women walked fast in all different directions, following signs to other buses, trains, the street, where I could see taxis lined up at the curb. Lots of people—men and women both—were wearing suits and pulling little briefcases on wheels, like tiny suitcases, behind them. Someone was making staticky announcements over a PA system. An old man in a motorized wheelchair chugged slowly toward the restrooms, holding a shivering Chihuahua on his lap.

"Now what?" I asked.

"Do you have your uncle's address?" Danny asked.

"Seven twenty West Flint Avenue." I had memorized it from all the letters Uncle Bread had sent me. "It's near a park."

We found a city map posted on the wall. It took us

a few minutes to find West Flint Avenue and more time to find the right train, called the Red Line. I was starting to feel sick again. We thundered out of the tunnel, into the twinkly thick of the night city, and my heart was like a jackhammer splitting pavement in my chest.

Even in the dark, I could tell that Uncle Bread's apartment building was four stories tall and made of brick. There was a low iron gate and, behind it, a courtyard. I could just make out the front door under a blue awning at the end. It was bitter cold and the wind rustled in the trees nearby, even though all the leaves had already fallen and lay in gray clumps on the ground.

"What's his apartment number?" Danny asked me, squinting at the row of buttons beneath the intercom to the left of the front door.

"Three ten."

Danny pushed the button, and I thought, *Maybe he doesn't want to see me, doesn't love me. Maybe that's why he left.*

A minute later, I heard Uncle Bread say, "Who is it?" in a tough, mean, city way. My heart beat fast, just hearing his voice.

"Uncle Bread?" I was going to say "It's me," but before I could get it out, the intercom crackled and Uncle Bread said, "Liv?" in the old voice that I remembered.

"Yes. Me and a friend."

"Oh, my God. *Jesus.*" Then he said, "Come up. Push the door when you hear the buzzer. Take the elevator to the third floor."

Inside, the lobby was plain, with a brown-tiled floor and two rows of metal mailboxes just inside the door. The smell was like a mix of the girls' bathroom at Dale Hickey Junior High after the janitor'd cleaned it and the chop suey from the Pagoda Palace on Mound Street. When we got on the elevator, I looked at Danny and whispered, "It smells funny," and he said, "That's what it smells like when you live next to other people." He said it like someone who knew everything about the world, who just wasn't going to be surprised, even if that elevator had stopped at the second floor and a dang zebra had gotten on.

But I could tell from the way he kept his eyes on the floor numbers over the doors that it was all an act.

On the third floor, I stepped out into the hall, and before I could say "Hi" or "I missed you so much," Uncle Bread was holding out his arms and saying, "Oh, my God!" and I couldn't remember if I started crying just then or if I'd been doing it quietly in the elevator the whole ride up and not even knowing.

"It's all right. It's all right," he whispered into my hair, and I couldn't stop shaking.

Then he picked me up, still hugging, and carried me

into the apartment. In the front hall, he put me down and kneeled in front of me. "How's my girl?" he said, and then I started crying again.

"Bless my soul," he finally said. "What we need is some Kleenex."

He disappeared for a moment, and I became aware that Danny was still standing out in the hall. "Well, come in. Come *in,*" I whispered loudly, waving him forward with my hand.

"You should introduce me," Danny whispered back.

"I will. Get in here, though," I said, irritated that Danny thought maybe there were politeness rules I didn't know.

Uncle Bread came back with the Kleenex. He was still thin, with red hair so pale it was almost pink. He had a half beard covering just his chin and upper lip: that was new. And his face looked older in some way that I couldn't pin down—not wrinkled, exactly, more like paper that had been crumpled into a ball and then smoothed out.

He was wearing green pajama bottoms and a gray Mizzou sweatshirt with the sleeves shoved up to his elbows. His bare feet were so white against the blue rug that I thought of clouds in the sky, the thin, wispy kind with no rain in them.

"Are you all right?" he asked. Without waiting for an answer, he handed me a tissue. "Now blow."

I wiped my nose and pointed out into the hall. "By the way, this is Danny."

Uncle Bread turned around and said, "Well, for Lord's sake," and held the front door even farther open. "Come on in, Danny. I'm so sorry. I didn't even *see* you."

Danny shuffled in, blushing. I wondered if he was thinking that it sucked to be another person in the same room with two people who already knew each other. Or maybe he thought Uncle Bread didn't see him because of how short he was.

Once Danny was inside, Uncle Bread closed the front door and turned back to us.

"Okay. In the living room *now,*" he commanded. Holding the Kleenex box to his side like a football, he headed through the archway, holding his other hand high over his shoulder and motioning that we were supposed to follow.

The living room walls were the color of a Band-Aid, not white like I was used to, and the floors were shiny, uncarpeted wood. I thought how cold it would be under your feet in the morning and wondered if maybe Uncle Bread was too poor to afford carpeting. But the furniture—two chocolate-colored suede love seats, a coffee table with wrought-iron legs and inlaid blue tiles on the table part, a flat-topped chest, and a metal reading lamp with a shade that looked like the stained glass in church—was unworn and unscuffed. Everything kind of matched, the way rooms in magazine pictures did. The lamp was on and cast low light like a candle.

Uncle Bread sat in the middle of one of the love seats, Danny and I across from him on the other.

"Hey, Uncle Bread, the fireplace is empty. Where are all the gorillas?" I asked.

"I gave most of them away. Olivia, what is going *on?*"

"Why did you give them away?"

He looked at me for a long time, thinking it over. "I gave them to a homeless shelter. For the kids," he finally said.

His answering me meant I had to answer him.

"I left," I said. "I had to."

"Why?"

I looked down at the floor, which gleamed like it was wet from a mopping. I wasn't ready to say everything.

"Olivia," he said again—still a serious teacher, not like the Uncle Bread who called me Jammie because bread and jam went together, "are you hurt? I mean, *hurt.*"

"No."

"Would you tell me if you were?"

"Yes."

"Well, then, what? What happened?"

It was too much to spill. I opened my mouth, but no words came out.

"Is it those damn pageants?" Uncle Bread asked, and before I could answer, he added, "How could you do this to your mama?"

"She called you?"

"Well, of course she called me. In case you showed up. She's going out of her mind."

"I left her a note. I told her I was all right, and that I would call her. Sometime. At some point in the, you know, future."

Uncle Bread folded his arms over his thin stomach and looked sideways out the window, into the blackness. Then he looked back at me. "That crazy old bat is just sick with worrying where you are."

If anybody else had called her a crazy old bat, I would have said something.

"I know," I said.

"I've gotta call her, Jammie. I promised I would."

"Uncle Bread, you can't. It's complicated."

"Not that complicated." He looked at Danny. "Is this your boyfriend?" he asked.

"No!" we both said at the same time.

"He's just a friend," I added. "He's on his way to meet his dad, who's coming back from Iraq. I told him he could stay with us."

Uncle Bread didn't say anything for a while. He just looked at us, from one to the other.

It is horrible when someone you love knows you're lying.

Horrible.

"Please don't call," I said.

He looked at us some more.

"If you call, we'll run away again," I said. "And then no one will know where we are."

I didn't recognize myself. What was happening to me?

"Three days," he finally said. "Three days and then I'm calling Jane. And your parents," he said, looking at Danny. "Three days."

After making us grilled cheese sandwiches, Uncle Bread set one of the love seats up for Danny to sleep on. He brought out blankets and a sheet and a pillow. From the guest bedroom, where I was changing into my pajamas, I heard him asking where Danny was from, how long his mom had been dead, how long his dad had been in the Marines. Every time I heard Danny answer,

I cringed a little. Then I heard Danny ask, "Can I call you Mr. Tatum?" and Uncle Bread laughed and said, "How about Fred?" and then something I couldn't hear. And then Danny said, "Danny. Danny's fine."

A few minutes later, Uncle Bread knocked on my door. When I said, "Yeah," he poked his head in and said, "You okay?"

By now I was in bed, barely able to keep my eyes open. The bed was made of dark wood and was queen size, which I knew because Imogene has a queen-size bed. It was covered in a white down quilt and was by far the biggest bed I'd ever lain down in, and just the size of it—knowing I could stretch out my arms and legs as far as they'd go and there'd still be bed under them—was enough to make me sleepy. The room was dark except for the light thrown by the bedside lamp, but in a cozy way. The bookshelf full of books made me think of libraries: hushed and safe. I thought, *Duh. Books* on a bookshelf.

Uncle Bread came in and sat on the edge of the bed. "Okay, Liv. No more bullshit. What are you doing here?"

After a minute, I said, "I'm so tired. Can I tell you tomorrow?"

"No. Now."

I couldn't face getting into the whole thing when I

could barely stay awake. "She was making me sing. For pageants. And I'm a terrible singer."

I knew if I said it was something about pageants, he would stop pestering me.

He shook his head. "Those damn freak shows." Then he was silent. I knew he was thinking bad thoughts about Mama.

"Have you read all those?" I asked, looking at the bookshelves, trying to get his mind off how awful Mama was.

"Yep. I love to read. I've got three or four books going on my bedside table. Those," he said, nodding at the bookcase, "well, some are from college. And high school, even. I never get rid of a book. I like knowing they're around."

"You and Daddy were different," I said.

"In some ways. Russell wasn't much of a reader."

"He liked football and playing pool and NASCAR." It was nice talking about Daddy to someone who knew.

"And doing cannonballs in the pool at the Trout Hollow Lodge at Lake Taneycomo. And sneaking out in the middle of the night to go ice fishing for bluegill at the pond on the Tesslers' farm. Jake Tessler didn't like for us kids to be fooling around on the ice, but Russell and Joe Steigler and Prescott Crowley and I got in and out before dawn. Usually caught enough for breakfast for all of us."

"I didn't know you liked to fish."

"I didn't. But Russell let me tag along. Did I ever tell you about the time he punched Prescott in the face?"

"I can't remember."

"For saying I ran like a girl. I thought he broke Prescott's nose, but he didn't. No one's ever looked after me like that. Not before or since."

We didn't say anything for a while, just stayed quiet in our own thoughts.

"So I gotta look after you, Liv, the way your daddy looked after me. You see that, right?"

"I'm okay."

"This isn't like you, honey. Sneaking away, scaring your mom."

"Maybe it *is* me. Not doing everything she says, for once. Doing what I have to, no matter who doesn't like it."

He looked at me a long time. "Your mama ever tell you you're a lot like your dad?"

"She says I look like her if she were thin."

"Well, you're a lot like both of them, then." He arranged the quilt around my shoulders so I was covered. "Three days, Jammie."

"I know."

"That boy? He's all right?" he whispered.

"Yes," I said. "Really."

"Well, sleep tight," he said, leaning forward and kissing my forehead. Then he said, "We're going to talk some more tomorrow. You hear me?"

I nodded, then closed my eyes and smiled at the dry scratchiness of his funny little beard. "Do you play chess?" I asked.

"I love chess," he said.

"Me, too," I said, my eyes still closed. I heard the click of the bedside lamp as Uncle Bread turned it off. I was going to ask if my daddy had liked chess, too, but before the words had arranged themselves in my mouth, I was asleep.

ten

I woke up smelling coffee and hearing the clatter of breakfast making. As I threw on my clothes, I noticed for the first time the window over the bed behind drawn white wooden blinds. I peeked through them and looked down onto the courtyard below. The sky was as gray as the twiggy trees. A woman was walking from the building out to the sidewalk. She was wearing a long quilted coat and a scarf wrapped over her chin and mouth.

"You gonna be warm enough in that?" Uncle Bread asked as I entered the kitchen. He was standing at the kitchen sink and eating granola.

I looked down at myself. "This isn't warm enough?"

"You need more than one sweatshirt. Just one and you'll feel like all you're wearing is a T-shirt."

"It's fine in Missouri in November."

"Missouri isn't Chicago." Uncle Bread rinsed out his bowl and put it upside down on the drain board. "Wear two. You can borrow one of mine. They're in my closet."

"Okay," I said, thinking, *No way in hell am I wearing two sweatshirts.* It would make me look thick and bunchy in the middle.

He was putting on a black leather jacket that had been draped over a kitchen chair. "Listen, Liv. I don't like the idea of you running around in a strange city. But I can't skip school. My kids are trying out for the fourth grade play. They need me."

I felt my face flush with anger. I thought, *Those kids see you every day!*

"I'll be fine," I said. The sound of my voice made him look up, but just as he was about to say something, Danny came in. I thought what a relief it must be for him, not having to wash his hair in a public bathroom sink.

"I was thinking maybe Olivia and I could go to the aquarium," he said. "I could get us there. I'm pretty good at reading maps."

"The Shedd? Well." Uncle Bread reached for a slim leather briefcase on the table. He looked uncertain.

"I got myself here, didn't I?" I said.

We looked at each other for a long time, neither of us blinking. I made myself not back down.

Finally he said, "You'll call me if you need me?"

"Yes. I will."

"You promise?"

"I *promise.*"

"Because it's a big city, Liv. It's not like Luthers Bridge. Things can happen."

Things can happen in Luthers Bridge, I thought but didn't say.

"What are you teaching today?" I asked, so I wouldn't ruin everything by sassing him, making him mad.

"Tsunamis and hurricanes."

"Don't you have to live near the ocean to worry about hurricanes?"

"It's good to know what they *are* no matter where you live." He zipped up his briefcase. "You ever been in a hurricane, Danny?"

"A couple times," he said. "But I live in an apartment. It just looked like a lot of rain."

"Can I make toast?" I asked.

"Yes. Hey, guys, I'm late. Here's a spare key, and here's a map. The Shedd's right here. Not far," he said, pointing. He was hurrying around, worried about being late. I thought about all the Dale Hickey teachers eating breakfast in the morning, getting ready to leave for work. I realized I'd never thought about that before. I sort of assumed that they just disappeared when school was over and magically showed up again at eight fifteen the next day.

I followed him out. He stopped at the front door.

"Be back by five," he said. I knew he wasn't kidding around.

"It's a big city, Jammie," he said again. "You be careful."

"I know. I will."

"You got my number?" he asked.

"Yes."

It was on the tip of my tongue to tell him everything—what was weighing on my heart—but he was hurrying and I thought, *Not now*.

"Okay, then." He checked his watch and stepped out into the hall. "See you tonight."

The door closed and I heard his key turning in the lock. And a little part of me felt hard and sealed shut, like it was me he was locking up.

"So the aquarium?" I asked Danny a few minutes later as we cleaned up our toast plates.

"Yeah. Sure." He scooted crumbs off the table into his cupped hand. "Only there's one other thing I have to do first."

"What?"

"There's something I want to see."

"Is it near the aquarium?"

"I have to check the map," he said.

While he studied the map, I realized it was pissing

me off, the way Danny was figuring stuff out alone, like I wasn't even there. "You could tell me, you know," I said. "Maybe I could help you find it."

"It's just a house," he said, squinting at the map, not looking up.

"Whose house?"

"Just a house! Jeez. Quit being such a frickin' pest."

"Listen, Danny. I'm not going to let you haul me all over Chicago like some five-year-old in a stroller."

We were looking at each other. In my head, I could hear the cartoon sound of someone slamming on the brakes, skidding to a stop.

"My dad's house," he said.

Out on the street, I finally knew I was in a strange place. I smelled coffee in Styrofoam cups and bus fumes and people hurrying. There was no silence. Birds sat in the empty trees along the sidewalk, but I couldn't hear them like at home. In summer these trees along the sidewalk would be thickly green and the air sweet and humid. I wondered if the birds sang then.

Uncle Bread was right about the cold. Fortunately, I'd brought mittens. Danny held the map in his bare hands, looking at it hard, as though it held a secret. He didn't even notice the woman with four little boys dressed alike in gray pants and blue parkas, or the old lady wearing an ankle-length gray wool coat and smudged pink Converse sneakers. People walked as though they really wanted to get where they were going.

On West Belmont, we passed Pedicute Nails and a public library and the House of Hookah Lounge. Our Lady of Mount Carmel Church made me homesick for New Faith Gospel. More bars, a hair salon, and a place where people did your taxes. We stopped at a Dunkin' Donuts: a cruller for me, a chocolate glazed for Danny. "For the train," he said, paying before I could get out my money.

We walked slowly past a video store, an army surplus, and a pharmacy, munching our doughnuts wrapped in paper napkins instead of saving them for later. Now the sidewalk was full of people walking the same direction, hurrying past us. A woman in khaki pants and heavy black boots knocked the rest of Danny's doughnut out of his hand as she accidentally bumped against him. I pulled off a piece of my cruller. "Here," I said, handing it to him.

We only had to wait about ten minutes before the train pulled up on the elevated tracks. We were headed north, away from the city, so there were plenty of seats. We found two in the front of a car. "How far are we going?" I asked, trying to see the city out of the scratched, sooty windows.

"Evanston. It's the first city after Chicago," Danny said. "We have to switch trains."

We rode the Red Line until Howard, which was the last station. I was worried that it would be complicated to switch trains. How many trains were there, anyway? How would we know which was the right one? Danny seemed to know, though. We rode a few minutes more. I was feeling sick from the doughnut and the closed-in air when the train chugged slowly to a stop. "We're here," Danny said. The second we stepped out of the car, I felt better.

Evanston was still a city, but different. Some of the sidewalks were made of soft, worn-out bricks. We saw lots of college kids, not so many old people, and no one in pink Converse Sneakers. "Now where?" I asked.

Danny looked again at the map. "This way," he said. "Toward the lake."

Now we were on a street thick with trees and lawns and houses that looked like castles. Mansions, Mama would have said. I wished I could have called her and told her. I would have said, "You wouldn't believe it." The kinds of houses you see in magazines or on TV. It was like elephants in the wild or Disneyland: something I knew was real but figured I'd never see. Three-story houses, all different from each other. Some of brick, with white shutters; some with stained-glass windows and towers and wraparound covered porches with matching furniture. One had huge bunny rabbits made of ivy in pots on either side of the front door.

"Your dad lives here?" I asked and it came out a whisper.

"I guess," he said.

We kept walking. No cars on the lawns or even on the driveways or parked at the curb. And no leaves on the sidewalk, although lots of the trees were bare. I wondered if leaves were like litter here. Everything was quiet, especially after Chicago. The only sound was of the soles of our shoes on the pavement. Nothing else, not even a dog barking. Were you allowed to have dogs here? At home, dogs barked all the time.

Finally Danny stopped and nodded at the house across the street. "That's it," he said.

It was enormous: made of gray stone, each window flanked by black shutters. A circular driveway curved around a perfect lawn so green it looked painted on. I wondered how they watered it; I looked for hoses and couldn't see any. I noticed, though, a red bike with training wheels leaning against the porch wall. It was out of place, the only thing that didn't go.

"You gonna knock?" I asked.

He was quiet a long time.

"No," he finally said.

We stood there for a while, him staring.

"Maybe we should go," I said. "Maybe they don't like you just standing around in this town."

"Okay," he said, but he stayed still for a minute longer, his eyes glassy, making me think of one of Mama's mule deer.

We decided to go to Navy Pier because I was hungry again and an ad at the train station said there were rides. We got pretzels at Auntie Anne's and walked to the east end of the pier. We sat under the flags—slapping in the wind like sheets on a clothesline—and looked out at Lake Michigan, which wasn't anything like Lake Taneycomo or Table Rock Lake. Lake Michigan was like an ocean. You couldn't even see across to the other shore.

"How long has it been since you've seen your daddy?" I asked, pulling off my mittens so I could hold my pretzel.

"Eleven years," Danny said. "He and my mom fought a lot. It was better that he left. Better for her. She didn't cry so much."

"My parents would have gotten divorced if my daddy hadn't died on the 475," I said. "Everyone gets divorced, practically."

"Yeah." Danny swallowed the last bite of his pretzel. "It's just . . . I don't get leaving. I get not wanting to be married anymore. I get not wanting to fight. I even get moving out. But leaving, really *leaving*. I don't know," he said, looking out across the silvery water.

"*You* left," I said.

"Yeah," he said, after a minute. "But if I could have gotten an apartment across town, I would have."

"So did your daddy get married again?"

"Yeah. To Susannah, who my dad says I'm supposed to call Mom when I write them thank-you notes. I'm not calling someone Mom when I haven't even met her."

"That would be hard."

"They have two kids. Liam and Abigail. Dad sends me pictures along with a check for my birthday. I think they're like ten and six. I think."

I tried to imagine what it would feel like to learn that Daddy had another family somewhere, with kids. In Georgia, maybe, where he drove his truck so much. I wondered if I would feel like they were my family, too, and decided I wouldn't.

"They're blond," Danny said. "They don't look like me at all."

"Did your daddy go to your bar mitzvah?"

"He sent a check." Danny wiped his mouth with his napkin. "He's an asshole."

"Then why were you looking at his house?"

"Just because, okay? Just because he's an asshole doesn't mean I can't want to see where he lives."

"Yeah, I know."

"I mean, your father's dead, right? But I bet he's buried somewhere and you go to the grave, right?"

"It's not a grave, exactly. It's a drawer. One of the worst fights Uncle Bread and Mama ever had was when he offered to pay for a headstone. Mama said no, even though she couldn't afford to do it herself. Uncle Bread said Mama was being pigheaded, and Mama said she had no use for college graduates who thought they were better than regular folks. Then she said, 'Mind your own damn business,' which I always remember, because Mama almost never swears. So Daddy ended up in an urn at the columbarium in Mount Jessup."

It was so easy to tell him things.

"Okay, well, whatever," Danny said. "You go there, don't you? And maybe talk to him a little? Or just remember things he said, things you did together?"

"Yes. I tell him how pissed off I am that he's dead. I say that even though Mama says he wasn't drinking, I'm not so sure. Just because I'm not so sure of anything, not because he drank that much. Not that I remember, anyway. But that's what happens when your daddy dies when you're four. You don't know anything for sure." I sighed. "If he'd lived and I'd had a normal growing up, I'd be surer about things."

He reached over and held my hand. Like it was nothing special, like we held hands all the time. Still looking out over the water, he said, "Going to my dad's just now was like going to a grave."

I was afraid to say anything, afraid to move. I wasn't cold anymore. I wanted us to sit like that forever.

"My mom works two jobs just so she can pay the rent," he said.

"Danny, I—"

"Dan," he said. "I think that would be better. I think I would like it more."

"Dan," I said, and just that—his new name on my tongue—made a shiver run through me.

"Come on," he said, standing up and pulling me with him. "Let's go for a ride."

eleven

THE amusement park on Navy Pier didn't have as many rides as the state fair in Sedalia, but I don't like to do too much spinning and whirling anyway. The only thing I really like is the Ferris wheel, and the one at Navy Pier was the biggest I'd ever seen. There was no line, so the ticket taker let us have a whole gondola to ourselves. Dan and I sat on the same side, close, me waiting for him to take my hand.

But he didn't.

The wheel started slowly and picked up speed, tossing us into the air, then holding us lightly as we fell. It took a few turns to get used to the way the earth arranged itself neatly as we rose and splattered into chaos and noise as we tumbled back down toward it. I settled into the rhythm—the magic of the up; the eyes-shut, dizzy down—and prayed in my head that even though I knew God had way more important things to do, would He please just let it go on and on, the up and down, me in this bubble with Dan forever.

Then the wheel started stopping, giving each gondola a chance at the top. "The buildings are so tall," Dan said.

"It's like they're people in a crowd, all different shapes and sizes," I said. "All pushing to be first. Or showing themselves off to us."

He laughed. "That's a funny way to look at it," he said, and I couldn't tell if he meant funny in a good way or a bad way.

When our gondola got to the top, I thought, *We found it, the one place in this whole dang city where it's finally quiet.* We just looked without talking, and it was like holding your breath: the stillness, the waiting for what would happen next.

When the wheel started to turn again, he said, "Do you think it's creepy when people who are different in age like each other?"

"I don't know," I said, but inside I felt as though he'd shoved my heart into a wood chipper and I was watching all the chopped-up pieces shoot out the back end.

"At my school, they think it's creepy," he said.

We didn't talk again, just sat as the wheel spun and stopped, spun and stopped, lowering us back to earth. We stepped out of the gondola, and the ticket taker looked me up and down the way some men do, probably thinking what I'd look like in a few years, or maybe even thinking about me now, which made me sick. But I smiled at him—something I never do with strange men—just to remind myself how pretty I was, how Dan was someone I didn't even know, some loser who couldn't even dream about kissing a girl like me. Just some short kid who played chess.

"We still have time for the aquarium," he said.

I was tired from all the running around, the trains and the walking, the tall buildings, the cold. But I didn't want to go back to Uncle Bread's, where we would be alone together and it would be obvious that we were just kids who had hitched a ride on the same bus, nothing more. It was only two o'clock, and we didn't have to be back until five.

Besides, I had never seen a whole building that was an aquarium. In my neck of the woods, people aren't so much interested in looking at fish as in catching and eating them.

"Fine with me," I said.

It was almost three by the time we got there. We wandered from room to room, each one walled with different tanks. I worried that the fish swam the same circles day after day and maybe missed the ocean, where they could swim straight if they wanted. But they seemed happy enough. Or maybe fish aren't happy; maybe they don't have enough brain to be happy. Maybe not being dead is good enough for them.

Asian arowana, bonnethead sharks, dwarf caimans, giant octopi. Anacondas and eels. Moon jellies. I loved the parrotfish, their colors like bolts of cloth at Turner's. We watched them for a long time in Waters of the World. They slipped past the glass, gnawing at coral, smiling their goofy, bucktoothed smiles at nothing.

"It says they poop sand," Dan said, reading from the plaque on the wall. I didn't answer, because boys only talk about poop with other boys or girls they don't really like.

We noticed the Australian lungfish lying like a log at the bottom of the tank. Granddad, he was called, the oldest fish in any aquarium in the world, at least eighty and maybe older. Speckled and dull, with a soft-looking snout. Unmoving. I thought, *What a terrible life.* But the plaque said that he had a primitive lung, that when the water was low, he would swim to the surface and gulp air into his mouth.

"I didn't know fish breathed air," I said.

"Only this fish," Dan said admiringly.

Next to us, two women whose little boys had pressed to the front of the crowd were gazing at the tank. One of them shivered a little. "That lungfish gives me the creeps," she said. "So ugly!"

"I don't like the way he just lies there," her friend said. "Can you imagine being at the beach and putting your foot down on *that?*"

"Jason, stop licking the glass!" the first mom called to her kid. To her friend she said, "I like the parrotfish more. So pretty! And the way they look like they're always smiling."

Dan moved on to another gallery, but I stayed watching Granddad for a while longer, trying to make up for the moms and their horrible, glass-licking children. I wanted him to know he was appreciated just for what he was, that he didn't have to swim around smiling.

We left the aquarium at around four. The gray afternoon was giving itself up to darkness and the cold was biting into my bones. We saw people clogging the stairs up to the train. "Maybe a bus would be better," I said.

We were studying the map when I looked up to see a policeman walking toward us, looking right at us. He was tall, with a round belly that hung over his belt: he took up all the space in front of me.

"You kids need some help?" he asked.

Dan talked before I could. "No," he said. "We're fine."

The policeman stared at us for a minute. "You from out of town?"

I nodded, and Dan said, "Yeah, our folks are waiting for us. At the hotel."

I knew the second he said it that he'd made a mistake.

"Which hotel?" the policeman asked.

Everything slowed way down; it almost seemed as though the other people on the sidewalk froze in their tracks. Then Dan grabbed me and started running.

At first I just followed, holding Dan's hand, ignoring the crowds of people we were dodging in and out of, keeping my eyes on him. I could hear the policeman behind us yelling, "Hey! *Hey!*" and I saw people noticing him and looking at us, but no one tried to stop us. I was sure I was going to get grabbed, but people just looked. Maybe it was a big-city thing. In Luthers Bridge, we would have been stopped for sure.

There were so many people. I'd never seen so many people except on television when there was a parade or a football game. Where had they come from? Then I realized they were flooding out of the buildings, that work was over and they were going home. "Come on!" Dan called, and I urged my feet faster to keep up. One block, then another. At the third, the light was red, and he pulled me to the left, across the busy street. I heard the policeman yell, "Hey!" again, but it seemed farther back than before.

"Run!" Dan said.

"What do you think I'm doing?" I asked, panting, thinking the word *run* in my head over and over, as if just thinking it would be enough to keep me going.

More crowds. Thank God the policeman was so fat. It was probably harder for him to get around all the people. Most of them didn't pay any attention to us, except for a lady in a bright green hat who held my gaze and asked in a loud voice, "Is this really necessary?" and a woman with a stroller who gave us a dirty look, like because we were running we had to have done something wrong and she didn't even want us on the same sidewalk as her baby.

Another block behind us. A bus pulled up to the curb; people grumbled and sighed, trying to board. Dan looked over his shoulder, past me, and then pulled me into the ragged line. "Pull up your hood," he whispered. My hand felt light and empty without his in it.

We climbed onto the bus and paid our fares. All the seats were taken. I held on to a pole and looked out the back window as we lurched into traffic. No policeman in sight. My heartbeat started to slow.

I looked at Dan. "Oh, my Lord," I whispered.

"Yeah," he whispered back.

The bus stopped and started, taking on more passengers than it let off. I began to feel sick and told

Dan. "We can't get off yet," he said. "Think of something else."

"Like what?" I asked. People who don't get carsick never understand that nothing helps except getting back on the ground again.

Just when I thought that I couldn't bear it for another minute, the bus jolted still and Dan grabbed my hand again. "Excuse us, please," he said politely, shoving us firmly toward the back door, and then we were out on the street. It was dark now, and colder, but I didn't mind. The wind, when it blew, felt like heaven, a relief.

"Where are we going?" I asked. The crowds were still thick, and I was tired and also hungry, the way I always am after I get over being carsick.

"I don't know," Dan said. "Maybe a movie. Someplace we can hide."

"I have to call Uncle Bread, though," I said. "It's almost six. He's going to be worried sick."

"We should get back to Uncle Bread's," I said. "It's almost six. We said we'd be back by five." The relief of the cold air was beginning to wear off; I was shivering.

He pulled me out of the stream of people, over to the metal security gate in front of a closed locksmith shop. He put his hands high on my arms, holding me still so I would look at him.

"Look," he said. "Your uncle thought we'd be back by five. He's probably called the police by now, which means if we go back to the apartment, he'll have to tell them we're there."

I nodded, realizing.

"They'll send us home," he said. "And I can't go back. There's stuff I have to do."

I shrugged enough so he had to move his hands.

"I don't want to go back either," I said.

We stood there, staring each other down. It was the longest I'd ever looked at anyone who was looking back. I thought maybe he was going to kiss me, and while I waited I thought how there are a few moments in your life when you are one person on one side of them and another person after you've crossed over, and how knowing that a moment like that is about to happen makes three seconds feel like three hours. I'd had only one moment like that before: the moment when Mama woke me up early one Sunday morning and held me in her arms while she told me about Daddy crashing his semi on the 475. This moment with Dan was different because I knew ahead of time that it was happening. And also because it was a happy moment, even with running away and the policeman and feeling carsick and cold, and now I was going to get to feel how I was different before and after something happy for a change.

But he didn't kiss me. He let go of my arms and said, "Okay, then," and I was still the same, still me, only a little different from what I was before: sad, let down, but not a-whole-different-person different.

"Let's get something to eat," he said. "Come on. There's Chinese across the street."

twelve

AFTER we ate—lemon chicken that tasted like chicken nuggets if you order the sauce on the side, and broccoli beef for Dan—we paid for tickets to a movie I'd never heard of, just to get out of the cold. Dan paid for everything, which was a little exciting, as though it was a date. The theater was wedged in between a sneaker store and a passport-photo developer, all part of a faded brick building that was the length of the whole block. The marquee was red with faded white letters running up to down, spelling PARK, lit up with twinkly white lights, the whole thing looking old, from another time. Some of the twinkly lights had burned out. Inside, the lobby smelled like buttered popcorn, but we didn't buy any because of all the Chinese food.

We sat in the middle of a row, close to the front, even though there were only a few other people in the theater. The seats were threadbare red velvet and not very comfortable, but I could tell as the previews started that I was almost asleep. It was so good to be warm and not moving, out of the wind, full of rice and chicken, with Dan, looking up in the dark.

I came half-awake a couple of times, once to music, once to the sound of movie gunfire. Usually I love movies in a theater: I almost never get to go, because of how expensive it is. Mama says TV is just as good and cheaper. But now I didn't even want to follow along with the story, which seemed to be about men shooting each other, running from someone. I closed my eyes and it reminded me of sleeping in my room back home, hearing the TV out in the living room, turned to the Food Network so Mama could watch cooking shows. It was comforting to fall asleep and know someone close by was still awake.

Something jolted my eyes open: the janitors were cleaning the theater and one of them had rolled the plastic trash barrel into the aisle and let it thump to a stop. I nudged Dan awake. "What time is it?" I whispered.

He checked his watch. I could see it said 10:20. "There's one more show," he whispered, "but we can't stay here. They don't let you stay without paying again."

We had sunk low in our seats so the janitors wouldn't notice us. "I have an idea," I said. "Just follow me out."

I sat up and made a big show of stretching and yawning. One of the janitors looked up from where he was vacuuming and said, "Movie's over. You gotta leave."

"Yeah, we know," I said. As we walked past him, I

smiled my best pageant smile and said, "Thank you." I wasn't thanking him for anything in particular, but janitors like to be thanked, and old people like it when kids are polite.

"You're welcome, young lady," he said.

Out in the red-carpeted hallway, Dan whispered, "Unbelievable."

"What?"

"Don't you see? How people are nice to you because of the way you look?"

"Yeah, I see." But something about his saying it pissed me off.

"So what's this big idea?" Dan asked, pulling up the collar of his jacket, getting ready for the cold.

"Go see when the last show plays," I said. "I have to go to the bathroom."

The women's restroom had two stalls and two sinks set in a marble-topped counter. No cupboards underneath, just bare pipes. There was a straight-backed chair with a ripped leather seat in the corner by the paper towel dispenser. I pushed open the stall doors. The toilets were the old-fashioned kind with lids and tanks. The bathroom was empty.

I went back out into the hallway. Dan was studying a framed movie poster. "The last showing just started," he said.

"Come here," I whispered, grabbing his arm and pulling him into the women's bathroom.

"Hey!" He yanked his arm away. "What the hell! I can't be in here!"

"Shhh! Whisper!"

"What's the matter with you?"

"I saw it in a movie once. We climb up on a toilet so our feet don't show under the door. And stay quiet. Maybe when they close up the theater, they won't know we're in here. We can sleep here."

He looked as though he wanted to argue. I quickly said, "It'll be warm."

"What if we get caught?"

"They'll give us a lecture and make us leave."

"What if they call the police?"

"Nobody's going to want to wait around for the police after midnight. It'll be easier just to kick us out."

"I don't know," he said, and I could tell he was the kind of guy who wasn't used to doing anything wrong.

"What do *you* think we should do?" I asked.

"I was thinking about riding the trains all night. Or maybe going back to the bus station."

"The trains will be noisy. And I don't think bus stations are safe. Plus, we'll stick out like sore thumbs. Someone might call the police."

He looked around, noticing for the first time the flowery pink wallpaper, the empty trash container.

"Is this what all women's bathrooms are like? Men's rooms aren't this clean. There are usually paper towels all over the floor."

"In women's bathrooms, too. Maybe this one's already been cleaned. Maybe no one will come back in."

"We should hide anyway. In case someone watching the movie wants to use it," he said. He pushed open the door of the second stall. "We should lock ourselves in this one."

"It's pretty small for both of us."

"Well, but we should leave one of them open. So if someone comes in, she can still use it."

"That makes sense," I said. Privately, I wondered if he wanted to be close to me, or if he was really just being logical.

It was pretty unromantic. Dan sat on the toilet tank and I sat below him on the closed lid, between his spread-apart legs. We locked the stall door. And then it just felt silly, and kind of embarrassing, being so close on a toilet.

"It smells better in here than in men's rooms, at least," Dan said.

It was embarrassing to talk about smells in a bathroom with a boy.

"We don't have to stay here very long. Just until the last show lets out," I said. "It's only another forty minutes."

"You know, I have to tell you," he said, and then stopped.

"What?"

"Just . . . you don't seem like the kind of girl who figures out how to get locked in a movie theater for the night."

"I'm not," I said. "Or I wasn't."

"It's cool," he said, "the way you figured out what to do."

I smiled.

Then he said, "I thought you were the kind of girl who always got your way, on account of how you look."

It was a compliment, I knew. But I couldn't help saying, "I can't help it if I'm nice to look at. I can't help it if I make people smile. Why is that a bad thing?"

"I didn't say it was a bad thing."

"Maybe it's because I know how to look people in the eye when I talk to them. Maybe it's because I know how to smile. Which, by the way, I learned in pageants."

"People should be nice to you even if you don't know how to smile."

"But they're not. Not always."

"Lots of people don't like the way their teeth look. Or are shy."

"People can be hateful," I said.

We were quiet. After a bit, I heard the roar of the vacuum cleaner, first loud, then a little softer, then loud, then soft from being pushed and pulled back on the hallway carpeting. I knew we were both thinking the same thing: that if the janitors hadn't already cleaned the women's bathroom, we were screwed.

"You don't know about hateful from personal experience," Dan said.

"My mama is really fat," I said. "I know about hateful."

The vacuum vroomed loud outside the bathroom door. I pulled my feet off the floor and hugged my knees close under my chin. We sat without moving, every inch of us stiff, afraid. The roaring stopped, and we heard a creak. Through the crack between the stall door and the stall, I saw the janitor poke his head into the bathroom and take a look around. I held my breath. Then, suddenly, it was dark. Not regular dark. Pitch-black, inside-of-a-closet dark.

"He turned off the light," Dan whispered. "Maybe everyone's going home."

But we were afraid to move, in case we were wrong. "Let's just sit awhile longer," I said. "Just to be sure."

In the dark, I was suddenly aware of Dan's legs on either side of me, his breathing above my head. It was weird to be sitting on a toilet in the dark, terrified to make a sound, terrified even to breathe, yet feeling so safe.

I think I fell asleep. I don't know for how long. The next thing I remember was his hand gently shaking my shoulder and him saying, "I think we're alone. I think I heard them locking the front doors."

I stood up, unfolding myself like a metal card table. Dan climbed down off the toilet tank and unlocked the stall door. We tiptoed into the hallway. All the lights were out, but dim light from the street trickled in through the glass doors: we could see shadows in the front lobby.

We looked at each other. I felt the worry drop away, like a heavy, wet coat I'd had to wear. No one would think to look for us here.

"This is better than the bus station," Dan said. "Free popcorn!"

I smiled, because it's every kid's dream, to be locked in somewhere you want to be anyway: an ice cream parlor, a toy store. But I knew we wouldn't gorge ourselves on candy or popcorn. I was too tired to be hungry, and Dan was too honorable to take something that wasn't his.

"We should stay away from the front doors. Someone might see in," I said. "I wonder if there are any blankets in this place."

We poked around a little behind the candy counter. No blankets, but there was a lost-and-found box with a couple of sweatshirts and a heavy winter parka in it. We carried the box to the auditorium and spread the sweatshirts on the carpeting at the wide spot in the aisle where people in wheelchairs could sit. We sat on the sweatshirts and Dan pulled the parka open and over us both. "To stay warm," he said. "They probably turned the heat off. It'll probably get cold later on."

We lay down under the coat, which smelled like someone else at first, and then stopped smelling like anything and was just something warm that covered us both. I lay on my back, looking up at the ceiling, which I knew was flat but which, in the darkness, began to look like an arched, black sky. I stared into it, imagining stars, the smudgy, faraway redness of Mars, a crescent of moon. And then I wasn't imagining it: I saw galaxies of stars, and smelled wet grass, and could just make out the shadowy shapes of trees, their leaves shielding all the birds from view. They would wait until dawn to sing.

It was still dark when I woke up, achy from the hard floor. Dan was on his side facing me, his arm thrown over me. I just lay there, wondering if his arm lying like that was an accident or not, and, after a while, I knew without looking that he was awake, too, watching me.

"Did I snore?" I whispered.

"No," he said, without moving his arm.

"Should we get up?" I asked.

"Not yet," he said.

I slept some more. The next time I woke, I knew it was close to morning. I was alone. He was probably in the bathroom. I stretched and felt the muscles in my back twist tight, like a towel being wrung out.

He came back with two Milky Ways and a medium Coke. Lowering himself to the floor, he said, "I left some money on the counter."

I tore open one of the candy bars. "What time is it?"

"Five thirty. I figure the theater opens around ten. The first show starts at eleven."

So we had a few more hours. "I don't even want to think about going back out there," I said. "I don't like that feeling of being looked for."

I didn't mind being looked *at*. Being looked *for* was different.

"Do you ever think about your mama? If she's missing you?" I asked.

"I know she's missing me," he said. "I don't let myself think about it."

"Do you think it would be different if you went back? If maybe she's learned her lesson? If she's ready to forget about the shots?"

"The thing is," he said, "I'm thinking maybe I might get the shots after all."

"Really?"

"It's just a few shots," he said.

"After everything you've been through?"

I imagined us holding hands, me looking up at him, him pulling me close as we walked, my head snuggled against his chest.

"I haven't decided," he said. "It's just something I've been thinking. What?" he said, seeing my face, which I knew looked disappointed.

"I don't know. I just think it's weird, you changing your mind like this."

"I'm not allowed to change my mind?"

I knew I wasn't being fair. "It's just an awful lot of trouble to put everyone through for nothing," I said.

"I told you to go home if you wanted. I *told* you!"

"I don't want to go home. I want . . ."

"What?"

"I don't want all this to be for nothing," I said.

"It's my decision," he said, crumpling the empty candy wrapper into a ball.

I couldn't think of an answer. It occurred to me that I really didn't know him very well.

"You know, that exit door probably just opens from the inside," he said. "We don't have to stay here. Maybe it would be safer to leave before anybody shows up."

"But where are we going to go?"

"There's something I have to do," he said. "You can come if you want."

In the bathroom, washing my face, I looked in the mirror and was surprised to realize that I hadn't looked at myself for two days. I leaned close in, really looking. I looked almost the same, just a little different in ways I wasn't sure anyone else would notice. Maybe from being in a strange city, or running away from a policeman, or spending the night somewhere I wasn't supposed to be, or not knowing what was going to happen next. It made me think that being born a certain way is only part of how you look, that everything leaves a trace.

A few minutes later, when Dan pushed open the exit door to the right of the screen, I stepped outside into the cold morning. I breathed in, loving the first breath, the shock in your lungs of outside air. "If we see a policeman, be cool," Dan said. "Don't run unless he looks like he's going to come over." I nodded, glad I had said I wanted to go with him, even without knowing where it was we were heading.

"I have something I have to do, too," I said.

He didn't say anything, just took my mittened hand, at first to steer me around a line of people waiting for a bus, but even after we'd gotten clear around them, he didn't let go.

We rode the train again. The trip seemed shorter in that magical way that all trips do the second time, when you already know the way. Changing trains this time was simple, a breeze; I didn't worry at all. It was still early—not even seven—and the sidewalks were wet. I couldn't tell if it had rained overnight or if somebody had watered all the lawns.

Some of the houses were closer to the street than the others. I tried to see inside them, but they all looked dark and shuttered up.

"Somebody must live in *one* of them," I said.

"What are you talking about? People live in all of them."

"Well, why aren't there any lights on? Why isn't anyone getting ready for school?"

"They are. You just can't see."

"Or making breakfast. Something."

"The kitchens are probably in the back."

I marveled about that as we walked: houses so big that you couldn't see the kitchen from the street. Even in Mrs. Drucker's house, you could see the kitchen window from the sidewalk.

"I wonder if you can smell bacon frying upstairs," I said. "I don't see what the point of bacon is if you can't smell it frying all over the house."

"Can we not talk for a while?" Dan asked.

I was all set to be mad, but he hadn't asked in a mean way, so I just stayed quiet.

Across the street, I noticed a woman walking the cutest little dog, a Chihuahua in a pink fur coat. The woman wore a gray coat over blue pajama bottoms and slippers that looked like moccasins except with fur in them. She stood patiently behind the dog, holding a plastic bag, which, I could see, was filled with dog poo. I wanted to laugh out loud. I thought about telling Dan, but I knew he didn't want to talk, so I kept it to myself, laughing in my head about the lady who walked behind her little dog collecting poo, like a really weird maid. Then I thought that that dog had a better coat than I did, and, even though it was still funny, I didn't want to laugh anymore.

When we stood again in front of Dan's father's house, I said, "Do you want me to wait out here?"

"No," he said, but still he didn't move.

"Why are we standing here?" I asked, trying to be gentle.

"I'm just rehearsing it in my head."

The house looked as unlit and unlived in as all the others. I counted six windows downstairs, three on either side of the double front doors, each framed in those black shutters, each with closed curtains. There were five windows upstairs, bedroom windows, I decided. There was probably a TV and a computer in each bedroom.

Dan said his daddy had a wife and two kids. Four people. What did they do with all those extra rooms? If the wife was anything like Mama, maybe she had a separate pantry for all her baking equipment and cookbooks. Maybe there was a living room and a family room both, and a separate dining room. Maybe a room for hunting trophies and a room for sewing and a room for reading, which seemed silly, because most people like reading in bed anyway, so why would you need a separate room?

"Okay," Dan finally said. He began walking down the long curved driveway toward the house. I followed a step or two behind, looking up at the second story to see if we were being watched, but the drawn curtains didn't move.

Now that we were up close, the lawn looked even

bigger than it had from the sidewalk. You could play soccer on it, it was so big, but there wasn't a single rut or gopher hole or mole mound that I could see. I wondered if you were lying on it in the middle of July, if it would have that amazing smell of sunny grass, and guessed probably not.

The front doors were tall and shiny black, each with a silver door knocker in the shape of a horse's head. The knocker part was like the bridle. Dan just stood there, looking up. I gave him a minute to rehearse some more. Then I said, "You should knock. He might have to leave for work soon," and Dan nodded and leaned forward fast and pressed the doorbell I hadn't noticed off to the side and I thought, *If you have two door knockers, what do you even need a doorbell for?*

We couldn't hear the bell in the house at all, not like at home, where you can hear when someone rings your neighbor's doorbell. Dan looked at me with his eyebrows arched in a now-what? kind of way, and I said, "Do you think you should press it again?" and suddenly there was the sound of metal sliding on metal and I saw him swallow and I forgot about myself, my own thudding heart, and focused only on him.

The door opened, and a thin, dark-haired woman smiled down at us and said, "Yes?" She was dressed in riding boots and breeches, which I knew from Imogene, even though Imogene only wore breeches for shows. Her hair was pulled back in a tidy ponytail, and she wore bright red lipstick and mascara and eyeliner. I had never seen an adult so made up so early in the morning. At pageants, the contestants sometimes have to report to the judges at seven with all their hair and makeup already done, but usually the moms look terrible.

"Uh," Dan said. He licked his lips. "Uh, is Gary here?"

The woman's face froze for a second, and then it seemed as if her eyes and mouth were scrambling to get back to normal. "Danny? Is that you?"

He nodded.

"My goodness, why didn't you call? Did your father know you were coming?"

"Not exactly."

"Well, dear. Gosh." She looked nervously behind her, and then back at us. "This is such a hectic morning—"

It didn't seem very hectic. No kids screaming or crying, and her all dressed, with her hair and makeup done.

"I'm sorry," Dan said, looking at his shoes.

I stepped forward. "We wouldn't mind waiting, if you think Dan's daddy would like to see him," I said, flashing my best pageant smile and looking right in her eyes, which in a beauty pageant is how you win but in real life is how you let people know you mean business.

"I'm just afraid that you wouldn't have time for a proper visit," she said, glancing down at her watch. "But I'll be glad to tell Gary to give you a call. He has your number?"

She was getting ready to close the door on us. I racked my brain, remembering how Mrs. Fogelson said to find a way to draw your subject out.

"Ma'am, can I ask you something?" I said.

She smiled a stretched-out smile at me, knowing there wasn't a good way to close a door on a kid who called you ma'am.

"What is it, dear?" she said.

"I couldn't help noticing your breeches, and I was wondering, do you give your horse cooked feed?"

She stared for a second, obviously caught off-guard.

Finally, she said, "Sometimes. My horses are primarily forage fed."

Horses. Plural.

"Are they pretty mellow, your horses?" I asked.

"As a matter of fact, they are." She smiled a little and crossed her arms. "They're pasture animals, you know."

"Oh, I know, I know." Thank the good Lord for Imogene always carrying on about Honey. "I've heard that horses that eat a lot of grain are more high-strung. Do you think that's so?"

"Yes. Yes, I do. As a matter of fact, I pay a lot of attention to what they eat. I tend to favor shredded beet pulp."

"What about sweet feed? What do you think about that?"

She started talking about protein and ADF values. I didn't pay any attention. I just nodded and crinkled up my forehead in an I'm-really-paying-attention kind of way and planned my next question, thinking that the longer she talked to us, the more likely it was that Dan's daddy would show himself. She babbled on. A southern accent. Maybe Kentucky, I thought, thinking of the Derby. She had thick fingers with short nails, unpolished. That surprised me. I just assumed rich women got manicures, maybe every day.

"I'm a big believer in linseed jelly," she was saying. "In moderation, of course."

Crazy. Plumb crazy. I know crazy horse people, people like Imogene who live and breathe horses, but this was different. Imogene is thirteen. This was a *mother.*

"Do your children like to ride?" I asked.

"Well, you'd think they would, wouldn't you? I

mean, it's in their blood. I come from a long line of horse people." She smiled modestly, as if she'd accidentally been bragging on herself. "But no. They're just not interested. They like their soccer, their gymnastics." She snorted a little, shaking her head.

She had just had a whole big long conversation with me and it hadn't even occurred to her that she didn't know my name.

Talking about her own children made her remember that we were standing on her front steps and that she wanted to get rid of us. "I'm sorry, but I really must fly. I hear the children now. And Danny, well, I'll tell your dad you were here. I'm sure he'll call you. How long are you going to be in town?"

I strained to hear. No kid noises of any kind that I could tell.

She had half-closed the door when, behind her, a man said, "Suzy, who's that? Who's there?"

Dan, who hadn't said a word during the whole horse conversation, looked up and said, in a hopeful way, "Dad?"

Suzy managed to glare at us and giggle at the same time. "Well, look who's here, baby," she said, pulling back the door.

Dan's father was dressed in a dark gray suit, the kind you never see men in Luthers Bridge wear, except at funerals. I couldn't help wondering if he was an undertaker. He was pale skinned and unsmiling and smelled like shoeblack, which made me look down. Sure enough, his loafers didn't have a scuff on them. He wore a white shirt and a blue tie. He looked like someone who did not care to bother with hugging.

"Danny. My God. What are you doing here?"

Dan looked up at him, and then I realized he was tall, maybe even taller than my daddy, who was a linebacker for the Horace Widener Mountaineers and was maybe more fat than tall, but still.

"I . . . I—"

"Are you all right?" his daddy asked.

"I have to talk to you," Dan said. He was rubbing his hands together, slippery with invisible soap. His nose was red with cold.

Dan's father looked at Suzy, who said, "Well, now, Gary, just look at the time!"

Then he looked back at Dan and said, "Come in, then," and Suzy kind of rolled her eyes and smiled in a fakey way and said, "Fine. *I'll* take them. It's not like this lesson hasn't been on the books for *weeks* now!" and flounced off.

We stepped into the front hallway, which was almost as big as our living room and dining room both, with a chandelier hanging from the two-story ceiling and a curved wooden staircase with carpet the same color as the bodice of my new pageant dress. Mama was right—burgundy does make you think of Christmas. I thought that, in a couple of weeks, Suzy was probably going to have a nine-foot Fraser fir delivered and set up right at the base of the stairs, lit in hundreds of little white lights like the trees at the Walmart Supercenter in Springfield, with maybe an electric train choo-chooing around the base all the time, so that whenever the kids came into the room, they could see it without having to press the start button first.

I wanted to think more about what Christmas would be like in this house—the piles of presents under the tree, in matching wrapping paper, not the *Luthers Bridge Morning Gazette,* the pine garlands running up the staircase, the smell of apple cider on the stove, or maybe, since this house was too big to smell like food, the smell of apple cider candles—but then I remembered that the Jacobsons were Jewish and probably didn't celebrate Christmas anyway. And then I noticed that Mr. Jacobson was staring at us both and saying, "What's this about, Danny? And who's this girl?"

thirteen

HE escorted us into a room off the front hall, paneled in dark wood and lined in floor-to-ceiling bookshelves. A room just for reading. I knew it.

Dan and I sat on the leather couch, but Mr. Jacobson crossed his arms and leaned against the corner of the desk, a way of staying above us.

"So? What's going on?" he asked.

Dan looked at the rug. "I ran away."

"Who's this girl?" he asked again.

"Liv. A friend."

I tried to smile, but it was so obvious something was wrong.

"A girlfriend? Is she pregnant? Is that what this is about?"

"Hey!" I said.

Dan put his hand on my arm. "No," he said to his daddy. "She's my friend."

I wanted to say something about being only thirteen, but then I thought it might not be such a good idea to draw attention to how young I was. Mr. Jacobson looked angry enough already.

"I don't get it. What's with you just showing up here all of a sudden? No warning, no nothing." Mr. Jacobson spread out his hands and shrugged his shoulders, like he was telling someone else, an invisible person in the room who would get it and take his side, how rude his son was.

"I didn't know I was supposed to *warn* you," Dan said.

"Well, then here's a word of advice, Danny. Here's something you can learn from me, okay? I mean, you're brilliant, you're a genius, you're goddamn Albert Einstein, but you don't know to call before showing up at my house at seven in the morning? Where one of my kids might just happen to open the door and want to know who the hell you are? Here's a tip, Danny. Call before just showing up. Can you do that? Huh?"

The air got very still. I was afraid to breathe.

"Sorry," Dan said.

"And don't go all sullen and misunderstood on me. What, you think you can just show up here, first time I see you in, what, ten years, and pull that teenage horseshit? No way, buddy. No goddamn way."

"Whose fault is that?" Dan's eyes were brimming with tears. "Who just left? Who called twice a year, on

Hanukkah and maybe my birthday, if you remembered? Who just sent money, like that was enough to make up for everything?"

He was really yelling. Usually, I hate yelling, but now I thought, *Damn right, asshole.*

"I asked you to go with me. I *asked* you. I tried. Come on, I said. It'll be fun, us boys on our own." His daddy was shaking his head, looking out the window. "Don't say you don't remember that!"

"I was four!"

"Are you saying you don't remember my asking you when you were six? And again, when you were nine? Is that what you're telling me?"

Tears ran down Dan's face. "I couldn't. I was all she had. And the only reason you wanted me was to get back at her. That's all you really cared about."

"Not true."

"Well, that's what it felt like. To me. You just asked once in a while to scare her, to let her know you hadn't given up, that she could never just relax, that it was always in the back of your mind. A possibility. And then"—he wiped his cheek with the flat of his hand—"you just stopped asking."

"You made your choice."

"Yeah. I did."

"And what was I supposed to do then? Keep asking

you? Beg? I *had* a family. I *had* kids. And at some point. Well." He looked out the window. "That had to be enough."

Silence. I studied the carpet, the intricate, interconnected weave of vines and flowers on the blue background.

"I could come now," Dan said, almost whispering.

Somewhere outside, I heard the sound of a leaf blower.

"No. It's too late for that," Mr. Jacobson said. "No. I'm sorry."

"God," Dan whispered, to just himself and me. Then, "Please?"

I knew it dang near killed him.

"What happened?" Mr. Jacobson said. "She getting to you? Showing her true colors?"

"Don't say anything about her," Dan said. "Don't say one word."

"Don't you be giving me orders in my own house!"

"You know what? I shouldn't have asked." Dan shook his head. "Never mind."

"You don't know," Mr. Jacobson said. Then he paused for so long that we both looked up. "How much I wanted you to ask me that."

I was stunned. People can say one thing and then

turn around and say another and you're thinking, *Wait a minute. What about that thing you just said a minute ago?*

You just don't know about people.

"Forget it," Dan said.

"For a while it was all I thought about. Getting you out of there. No, really," Mr. Jacobson said, seeing Dan's face. "It was.

"But after a while, I stopped asking, because you'd made up your mind. And then I stopped thinking about it, because it was settled, and, you know, how much can you torture yourself with something? At a certain point, you have to take your marbles and go home."

I thought of the marbles in Turner's General Store, plunging my hands into the full bin of them, pretending their coolness was water.

"And now." He was looking just at Dan. "Things are—well, you know. Up in the air."

"Forget it, I said."

"She's halfway out the door. And I've got to worry about the other two. She wants them. And I work for her father. Jesus," he said, a hand on each thigh, holding himself up, but head down, sagging with the weight.

Dan swallowed. "It's all right, Dad."

"Jesus," he said again. "But you know, it's just too hard right now. To accommodate something like this.

Everything is very fragile. Even you just showing up. It's put me in a very awkward position."

Dan stood up, so I did, too. "Okay," he said. "Okay."

Mr. Jacobson leaned around and opened the desk drawer. He pulled out a checkbook.

"No, don't," Dan said.

"No?" Mr. Jacobson put the checkbook back and stood up, then reached into his pocket for his wallet. "Take this, then. Take something," he said, holding out a small wad of bills.

Dan took the money and stuffed it into his pocket. I knew he was thinking what taking it meant: that he was forgiving his father, saying everything could go back to the way it was, and hating himself a little for it.

At the door, Mr. Jacobson said, "I hope you understand."

Dan nodded with the smallest possible movement of his head, the way a man does, not letting anything out.

"You going to be all right? You got a place to stay?" Mr. Jacobson asked.

"Yeah."

"Well." Out of questions to ask, things to say. He smiled, ready to let it go at that, and I thought, *A real daddy would want to know where.*

He held out his hand to me. "Nice to meet you, Liv."

I shook his hand and said, "Thank you," knowing Dan wouldn't want me to make a scene.

"Danny?" he said.

Dan looked at the outstretched hand and then met his daddy's eyes. "It's Dan," he said, keeping his hands jammed deep in his pockets.

"Well." Mr. Jacobson flushed. He pulled open one of the massive front doors. "I'll call you."

We stepped out into the deep, gray morning cold.

"You know how to get back to the station?"

Dan turned around and nodded yes, his chin just barely tilting up.

"Safe travels, then." And he disappeared behind the closing door.

We hiked back out to the sidewalk on the gently curving driveway. I looked Dan's way, but he kept his eyes straight ahead. "Asshole," he said, his breath a cloudy puff of steam.

On the train, he said, "Do you think it was bad I didn't shake his hand?"

"No."

"You think maybe I should have said I was sorry for not calling first?"

"No."

He kept his eyes on the passing landscape: cars spewing exhaust, the ghostly trees. “I don’t even know those two kids and I feel sorry for them.”

Everyone has something horrible in life to get over: a mean daddy, a dead daddy, being short, singing lessons. Not being beautiful. I said, “They’ll be all right. Nobody’s going to have to work two jobs, paying for things.”

“I still feel bad for them.”

“They’ll be all right.”

“You don’t know that.”

“I guess,” I said, letting him be sad, because that was what he wanted. But I was thinking that they *would* be all right because most people are, eventually. And that struck me as amazing—staggering—the kind of thing you can think a million times and not even notice and then think once more and be shocked.

Later, as the train slowed at the Belmont station, I said, “What do you want to do now?”

He puffed out his cheeks, sighing, tired. “I want one of those pretzels.”

“That sounds good,” I said. The train doors whooshed open, and a few people entered the car, the cold on their coats. “We have to watch out. There are a lot of policemen down there.”

"Yeah, I know," he said, and I could tell from the way he said it that he was almost done, too tired to care.

Navy Pier was now a place I knew, a place I was coming back to. The lady at Auntie Anne's smiled as she handed me my sour cream and onion pretzel. "I think she remembered me," I said after we paid. It felt good, being remembered. It made me think of Chicago in a different way, as thousands of Luthers Bridges that just happened to be close together, each one full of people who could be neighbors, friends.

We smiled at the man dressed in a dog costume, wearing pirate clothes and an eye patch, patting little kids on the head with his big paw-hands. I saw a couple of policemen as we strolled along, but they didn't pay any attention to us. "Maybe they've stopped looking for us," I said.

"Too many real criminals," Dan said. "And they weren't looking for us. They were looking for *you*."

I was going to argue with him, but then I thought, Maybe Dan's mama was like his daddy, not really wanting to know where her boy was, glad it wasn't her having to be responsible. Without thinking, I grabbed his hand and held it. He didn't say anything, but he closed his eyes for a second, reminding me how long his lashes were, and that, even though he didn't want to be found, there was pain in not being looked for.

I knew we were heading to the Ferris wheel without either of us having to say so. In the gondola, we sat close together, holding hands, facing forward, both of us tipping our heads up at the sky as we started to move. We climbed and climbed, and there was a second at the very top that was like taking a breath, and then we skidded around and down. I was dizzy with joy, with not thinking, not wanting anything else except this.

Then the wheel began stopping, letting each car have a turn at the top. I missed the moving, the flying feeling, but I knew we were heading toward the highest point. It reminded me of Carson Jeffries painting New Faith Gospel, sitting on top of the scaffolding at lunch, seeing Luthers Bridge in a whole new way.

"It was really good today, the way you talked to Suzy," Dan said as we lurched upward. "It was amazing."

"Thanks."

"If you hadn't done it, I never would have gotten to talk to him."

"That's why I kept talking. I don't usually do that."

"I know. I just wanted you to know I knew." He paused so long that I turned to look at him. He said, "The reason I'm thinking about getting the shots is that

I thought, maybe, you might like it if I did. If I was taller."

"I don't care anything about that," I said.

He kissed me. He kissed me for so long that, when he finally stopped, I realized we'd already had our time at the top and were heading back down to earth.

"We missed it," I whispered, not even caring.

"Let's go again," he whispered back.

We rode the Ferris wheel for over an hour, until it started to rain and the operator made us get off so he could shut the ride down. The pier was almost deserted. We ducked into King Wah to get out of the rain and ordered pot stickers. We found a table in the back corner and sat next to each other. The pot stickers were sweet. When he kissed me, his lips tasted like soy sauce.

"We can't stay here too long," I said. "Two kids kissing. Someone's going to complain."

"I don't care," he said.

So much happiness. I thought I would burst from being so full with it; I had to smile just to let some of it out. It was the happiest I'd ever been. Winning pageants? That wasn't happiness. Now I knew.

"But I have to go back to Uncle Bread's," I said. "Even if the police are there. Even if he calls my mama."

"I know," he said.

He didn't know, not really, but he said it as if the only thing he was thinking about was making me happy, doing what I needed him to. I kissed him again and knew that we were coming up on the end, whether we wanted to or not. And I thought that, for the rest of my life, that was what the taste of soy sauce would remind me of: a mixing on my tongue of happiness and the knowing that happiness can melt away in an instant, leaving just the slightest hint of itself behind.

It was almost dark when we got back to the apartment. I let myself in with the key Uncle Bread had given me. He wasn't home. I went into the bathroom and toweled off my wet hair. In the mirror, my skin looked pink: rain washed, scrubbed clean.

When I came back to the living room, Dan was sitting on one of the love seats, waiting for me. He'd turned on the lamp. The low yellow light warmed me like fire. I settled in close to him and we kissed a little, but not the way we had before. Now it felt like gratitude.

I heard the key in the lock, the door pushed open, Uncle Bread saying, "Liv! Is that you?" Before I could say "Yes," he'd come into the room, still holding his briefcase, water dripping off his raincoat. "My God, Liv!" he said, dropping the briefcase, pulling me into a hug. "You scared the shit out of me!"

"I know," I mumbled into his wet shoulder, "I know. I know," a part of me wanting to say *I'm sorry,* but I wouldn't let myself.

Finally, he pulled away and said, "Oh, God. Look at me dripping all over you." I went into the bathroom to use the towel again, and when I came out, he had taken off his raincoat and was sitting across from Dan, who was saying, "We're fine. Really."

"But where did you go? Where were you?"

Dan looked at me, not sure if he should say. And I realized I didn't want him to, that I wanted our night in the movie theater to be just ours, something only we knew. I wanted to be able to remember it when I was an old lady and know that, somewhere out in the world, Dan was remembering it, too, and that it was just us.

"Liv. Dan. I want an answer."

He said it as though we were kids who'd lost our backpacks or come home after curfew. And I didn't feel like a kid. I was someone who'd kissed a boy I really, really liked, who had just made a memory that would last me all my life. I didn't need to be lectured or given a talking-to. I felt a wave of anger wash over me.

"Uncle Bread, I need to talk to you," I said. "Alone."

fourteen

UNCLE Bread closed the door to the guest room and looked at me like, *Do you have any idea what you've put me through?*

I opened my mouth, but nothing came out. Suddenly, I was speechless. My nerves gave out.

He sat down on the straight-backed chair across from the bed. He looked pale and weary. "Does this have anything to do with you disappearing last night?" he asked.

"Not exactly—"

"Because I have yet to hear an apology. And I would like to hear one."

I had never seen him angry at me before.

"Do you have any idea what last night was like? The worry? Wondering if you'd been hit by a bus? Kidnapped? If you were dead? Do you have any idea?"

"Okay, okay. I'm sorry."

"Olivia." He got up and sat next to me on the bed, scooching up close and taking my hands. "This is so unlike you, scaring people. What is the *matter?*"

I jerked my hand away. "Nothing. And I said I was sorry. What more do you want?"

"I want to know what's going on."

"Why does something have to be going on? Why can't this just be me being a normal girl?"

"Do you think normal girls run away from home without telling their mothers where they are? Or their uncles?"

"How would I know? How would I know what normal girls do?"

He leaned back, away from me. "Oh-h-h-h," he breathed, as if the whole thing were dawning on him.

"What?" I said, irritated that he thought I was so easy to figure out. Just one more box to be put in. "Look, this isn't about pageants."

"Well, what, then?"

"Not everything in my life is about pageants!"

"Okay. Okay," he said soothingly, but it was too late: I was already crying. Sobbing, holding my face in my hands. "Shhh. It's all right, Jammie," he said, rubbing my back.

"Quit doing that," I said, arching away from his hand. "And don't call me Jammie."

He took his hand away and sat quietly while I cried. I couldn't stop, even though I knew crying made me look ugly. But I didn't care. I couldn't stop thinking about the dresses. The evening gowns and the costumes, the organza and the tulle, the bows and lace. So many dresses. When I got a new one, I couldn't wait to wear it. Stiff and sparkly, it crinkled with the magic of possibility. I couldn't wait. And then, after I wore it, it was just a dress. Mama would sell some of them on eBay to help pay for another one. Gone. Now it seemed like such a waste.

Maybe I wanted to look ugly right now.

I hiccupped and wiped my nose on my sleeve. Uncle Bread reached for a box of Kleenex on the bedside table and held it out to me. After I blew my nose, he said, "Your mom will understand, Olivia."

"Understand what?"

"About the pageants. That you don't want to do them anymore. She might pitch a fit, but she'll come around."

"I know that." His being on my side was getting on my nerves. "That's not why I'm crying."

"Why, then?"

"It's just . . ." I sighed, exhausted. Crying is hard work.

"I know your mother. She doesn't like being thwarted. She can be scary. But I'll help, if you want. We'll tell her together. Don't you worry about it," he said, putting his arm around my shoulders and pulling me close. "I'll stand by you."

"Oh, really? Is that what you'll do?"

He let me go.

"You're not going to stand by me. That's a lie," I said. "Maybe what you meant was that you'll *send me a letter*."

He didn't answer. He crossed one leg over the other and watched it bounce up and down.

"That's what you meant, isn't it? And you'll write all kinds of good things. You'll say how you love me and you're proud of me and how everything will work out!" I was yelling now. "And how busy you are with all your kids at school! How *amazing* they are!"

"Liv. I'm sorry."

"Sorry for what? You don't have anything to be sorry about." The more I yelled, the more my insides burned.

"Just . . . sorry. I'm sorry," he said. "I'm sorry for everything."

"You know what I remember? How Valentine Biswell got run over by a Subaru Forester."

Uncle Bread sighed.

"I got three whole letters about that. How someone else's mama accidentally backed over her foot in front of the Augustus Hodge School and carried Valentine into the front office even though she wasn't crying or screaming or anything because she was so *brave.* And how she had to stay home for a week because her daddy didn't have enough money for pain pills, and how you bought her Children's Tylenol with your own money, and visited her every day after school and brought handmade cards from all the other kids so she would know how much they all missed her."

"I wanted you to know what my life was like. You were important to me. I wanted—"

"Why did you leave?"

Everything in my body was on fire, the sobs in my throat like flames.

I cried until I couldn't cry anymore. When it was over, I had no bones, nothing to hold me up. He put his hand on my back; my skin hurt. Everything was sore and tender.

"It was complicated," he said. "It was too much for a four-year-old to understand."

"I wanted to be Valentine Biswell, all bent up with pain, hobbling around on crutches, not being a very good reader anyway, and now being even worse with all the school I'd missed. I didn't care about any of that," I said. "I just wanted to be her."

"I'm sorry," he said again.

"I hated Valentine Biswell. For years. I had the meanest thoughts. That she must have been retarded, being a slow reader. That she wasn't brave for not screaming—she just liked all the attention, everyone fussing. And that her daddy . . . Well. How at least she *had* a daddy." I paused. "I liked to pretend that she was ugly, really ugly, the kind of ugly where kids whispered nasty things and teachers were hateful to her because they knew the other kids didn't like her and they were trying to win them over." When he looked at me funny, I added, "Teachers do that, you know."

"I know," he said.

I reached for another tissue and blew my nose hard. Then I asked, "Was she?"

"Was she what?"

"Ugly."

He ran one hand over his scalp.

"It was a long time ago, Liv. Seven or eight years." He met my eyes and said, "I think she was a perfectly nice-looking girl. A nice, average-looking girl."

I felt better. If you're ugly, people feel sorry for you. In a way, it's worse to be average looking than to be ugly.

"So explain it to me now. Why you left," I said.

"It's still complicated."

"Was it because you're gay?"

Uncle Bread look shocked for a moment. Then he burst out laughing.

"I'm not gay," he said. "Where'd you get that idea? Oh, wait, don't tell me. Janie?"

"Well, yes." I was embarrassed to be so wrong. Then, when the embarrassment wore off, I was shocked. For the second time in one day, I thought, remembering Dan's daddy being crazy and mean one minute, sad and rejected the next. Sometimes I went for weeks not even being surprised.

Uncle Bread laughed again, but sadly. "Your mama is a piece of work," he said. "Talking shit about someone she doesn't know at all. Making up stories."

"She said you were gay and you had to leave Luthers Bridge because there were no other gay people for you to hang out with. And that, if you'd wanted to, you could have taken a class or something and learned how to like girls."

"When did she say all this? When you were *four?*"

"No. I don't remember exactly. She used to mention it every once in a while. I think she wanted me to stop missing you so much and she thought . . . maybe . . ."

"That if you thought I was gay you wouldn't love me anymore?"

I nodded yes. Then I said, "It didn't work, though."

"Thank you for that, sweet Liv." He turned my shoulders so I would face him. "Gay people are just gay. They're born that way. It isn't anything to be ashamed of."

"Okay." I pretty much knew that anyway.

"They can't take a class, and why should they? There's glory in being who God meant you to be. And as for me, well, I've been hearing things like this my whole life. If you're a skinny boy who doesn't like sports and likes to read, you hear it all the damn time. You get awful tired, after a while." He shook his head. "So I left because I wanted to live somewhere crowded with people. So that, even if there were still a lot of people who were like your mother, there'd be a few who weren't. Who'd get me. Who'd see who I really was. That answer your question?"

"Yes," I said. "It does."

I felt everything slowing down, the way it does after you've yelled. Or when something that seemed crazy finally starts to make sense.

After a minute, I said, "Dan says some kids talk baby talk to him. He says he doesn't mind, that he's gotten used to it."

"I bet that's just what he says."

"Maybe."

"You don't really get used to it. You *cope*. You *adjust*. But after a while . . ." He paused. "You get pretty sick of the whole damn thing."

I thought about Mama being fat. There are no shots for that.

"What happened to Valentine Biswell?" I asked.

"Last I heard, she was struggling in high school. Running with a rough crowd."

He looked sad.

"I'm sorry," I said.

"Yeah." He sighed. "You do what you can, you know? And when it isn't enough, you feel terrible. Terrible."

We sat for a moment, in the soft, buttery lamplight, Uncle Bread looking as though he'd lost a race, me thinking that, as it turned out, I was glad not to be Valentine Biswell.

Finally, I said, "I'm sorry for the rest of it, too."

He reached for my hand. "You know what you've got to do now?"

He meant call Mama. "I know."

"And Dan. I can't let him stay here. And I can't just turn him loose, to roam the streets. That's not a way to live."

"I know."

"There are good social workers out there, people who can help him."

"Let me talk to him first. Please."

He leaned forward and kissed me on the forehead. "Your daddy—"

"Don't say anything about him being proud of me." He wouldn't have been proud of the way I'd run away, how I'd put Mama through holy hell.

"I was going to say he was a good talker, too."

I walked into the living room, and Dan knew immediately. "You're going back," he said.

"I have to." I sat next to him on the soft suede love seat. "Don't be mad."

"I'm not."

"You look mad."

"Quit picking at me." He turned away, toward the fireplace. "This is just how I look."

I put my hand on his back. "What are you going to do?"

He was silent for so long that I thought maybe he hadn't heard me. But finally he said, "I have an aunt in Denver. She'd let me live with her, I bet." He paused. "There'd be snow," he said.

I laid my head against his back and put my arms around him. "Please don't do that," I whispered. "Please go home."

We just sat, not talking. I wondered how long it

would be before I felt like putting my arms around a boy again.

"She'll make me get the shots," he said.

"Tell her this is how God made you."

"It won't matter," he said miserably. "She won't pay any attention."

It made me think of the Boston Tea Party, the Massachusetts colonists standing their ground, disguising themselves as Indians, boarding ships in the cold autumn night. The harbor water stained brown with tea. Coercive acts.

"Just because you live with her doesn't mean she can tell you what to do," I said.

He half-turned to face me.

"If I did get the shots, what would you think?" he asked.

I let him go, studied his face. I could see there that it mattered to him, really mattered, what I thought.

"That you wanted to make her happy," I said. "And maybe that you wanted to be happy, too."

He hugged me hard. I could feel him shaking. I couldn't tell if it was from crying or relief. Maybe I was shaking a little, too.

fifteen

I called Mama. "Don't cry," I said over and over again, but she couldn't stop, even when I said I was fine, I was with Uncle Bread, everything was okay. "I'm coming home," I said, and she blubbered, "I'll say you are," but she didn't sound mad at all, just weak and relieved.

When I got off the phone, my own tears welled up. I had known she would be afraid, but it was one thing to know it and another thing to hear it in her voice and in her sobs that just kept coming.

We stayed one more day in Chicago. Uncle Bread took a sick day to show us around. His girlfriend, Heidi, came along. She didn't have to take a sick day because she was a writer and could do whatever she wanted and work at night.

"What do you write?" I asked.

"Vampire novels for fun, obituaries for money," she said. She was pale, with dark, curly hair pinned up in back except for two perfect tendrils spilling down around her face. Her eyebrows could have used a little tweezing. She wore ripped boyfriend jeans and a black turtleneck under a black velvet blazer, bright red mittens, and a pink paisley scarf at her neck. She wasn't pretty the way I was used to, but I couldn't stop sneaking looks at her as we rode the elevator down to the street.

We had waffles at Sam & George's, then rode the El downtown to the Willis Tower. "It'll always be the Sears Tower in my book," Uncle Bread said. Then he added, just to me, "That's what it used to be called."

"You old fuddy-duddy," Heidi said, nudging him with her hip, then curling into his side for a hug.

He put his arm around her shoulders. "Damn right," he said. "If it were up to me, Badfinger would still be called the Iveys."

"What is Badfinger?" I asked.

"A band," Uncle Bread said, and then he and Heidi laughed at how it was weird that they knew such an obscure fact. And I felt happy that they had each other.

We stood on the busy sidewalk, looking up.

"I ain't never seen anything so tall," I said, and then felt ashamed, that I'd said *ain't,* which I almost never said, that I was showing what a hick I was.

"It's amazing, isn't it?" Heidi said. "I grew up here and I never get tired of looking at it."

Dan stood next to me, head tipped back. I wished he would take my hand.

"Do they have buildings this tall in Houston?" I asked.

"Not quite," he said.

We rode the elevator to the 103rd floor, the Skydeck. It was like being in space and looking down. Last night's rain had disappeared; the sky was as blue as toothpaste, cloudless, vast. Below, the skyscrapers that had seemed so tall from the street looked like building blocks, and all of Chicago stretching out in all directions like a city made of Legos.

"It doesn't look real from this high up," I said. "It looks like a picture of a city."

"Look," Dan said, pointing. "Navy Pier!"

It was so different from up here: gray roofs on a tiny spit of land, your eyes drawn to the endless lake. I couldn't even see the Ferris wheel. Something I would dream about, but invisible from the air.

At first I was afraid to stand on the Ledge. There were four of them: glass boxes that extended from the side of the building. But when Heidi and Dan climbed out into one, I felt like a baby, being afraid.

"You won't catch me out there, either," Uncle Bread said. "No one's going to blame you for wanting to keep both feet on an actual floor."

"But I *don't* want that," I said. It sounded like whining, but still I couldn't move.

"Wow! Oh, my God! *Wow,*" Dan was saying, peering between his feet, through the glass to the faraway street below, and I thought, Which would be better: feeling safe and disappointed in myself, or getting to see *that?*

I climbed out onto the glass floor, my legs wobbly with fear, and looked down. The street below was clogged with cars, small trucks, yellow taxis. It ran along the river, a sludgy green. A short ways off, a freeway curled over and under itself like smoke. Looking down felt like flying, maybe. Or maybe like being dead and watching the earth from a cloud. Was that what my daddy saw? Did he watch me from wherever he was? Could he pick me out?

"Kind of puts things in perspective, doesn't it?" Heidi said, and even though she couldn't possibly have known what I was thinking, it made me nervous, made me wonder if something was showing on my face that I didn't mean to be there.

We were hungry again. After getting chili dogs, we caught a bus to the zoo in Lincoln Park. "I've never been to a zoo," I said, afraid I was looking like a hick again, but all Dan said was, "The snakes are my favorites," and Uncle Bread said, "I have an affinity for the great apes," which made Heidi laugh loudly and kiss him on the shoulder.

I loved the animals at the zoo, but I had a nervous feeling as we stood outside their cages, waiting for them to wake up, eat, wrestle, pace. "I wish they were in the forest, where they belong," I said to Uncle Bread as we stood with a small crowd of people in front of the gorilla enclosure, watching a sleeping silverback.

"There are poachers in the wild," he said. "They're safe here."

But it didn't make me feel any better. "It's like everyone wants to be entertained," I said. "How can they just live if they're supposed to be putting on a show?"

"They *are* living," he said. "This is all they know."

The old gorilla stretched and rolled himself up to a sitting position. He met my gaze and then, bored, turned his silvery back.

The zoo closed at 4:30, which gave us just enough time to take a train out to the airport. Dan's mom was paying for him to fly home. "Lucky!" I'd said, but Dan had shrugged. "I flew to New York a couple of times with my grandparents," he said. "It's no big deal." I hardened my heart a little, thinking, *See? He doesn't get you. He's just some boy.* I knew it was a lie I was telling myself.

At the airport, Uncle Bread and Heidi went off to find the bathrooms, leaving Dan and me in the check-in line. *Our only time alone,* I thought, and, as if he read my mind, he set his duffel bag on the floor and grabbed my hand. "I don't want to go," he said, pushing his bag with his foot as the line inched forward. "I don't want to leave."

"I know."

"Leave *you.* I don't want to leave *you.*"

I nodded. "Maybe you can visit. And you've got my e-mail address."

"You know that won't happen. The visiting part."

I knew. I wanted to think it might be true, though.

"We can play chess online, if you want," he said. "There are programs."

"I'd like that," I said, even though I wouldn't really, because it wasn't romantic. I could play chess with anyone.

I stood with him while he checked his bag and got his ticket and seat assignment. Then we had to say goodbye for real: only passengers could go through the gate.

"Where's your uncle?" he asked, craning his neck.

"I think they're letting us say goodbye."

He took both my hands, made himself look me in

the eyes. "You've probably kissed other guys," he said. It was really a question he was asking.

I felt myself blush and decided that would be my answer.

"I . . . I . . ." He blushed, too, a dull red stain spreading down his neck, making me want to put my lips there, to feel the warmth that way. But I didn't. It would just make everything harder.

"I know," I said.

"I won't forget. Ever."

I smiled. "I never spent the night on the floor of a movie theater before."

"I won't forget that, either."

"It was—" But I didn't want to try to put it in words, how I thought I would think about that night forever, maybe walking down the aisle at my wedding, maybe as I sat up in the middle of the night, trying to get my baby to sleep in her crib. It was the night everything changed, was made clear, the night I knew how to fix things, what to do. "Great," I said. "It was great."

"It's probably the only time I'll ever do *that,*" he said. "Both of us, probably."

Then he kissed me goodbye and it was like all that time on the Ferris wheel: the world dropping away to nothing, spinning.

★

Uncle Bread put me on the bus early the next morning.

"Are we all right? You and me?" he asked.

"I'm still mad," I said. "But yes."

"I'm so sorry, Liv," he said. "I'll always be sorry for that."

"Not so mad anymore," I said.

He kneeled down in front of me as though I were a little kid. He hugged me. I laid my head on his shoulder, smelling his coat, taking in an easy breath, filling my lungs with loving him and being only a hint of angry.

"You tell Jane to behave herself," he said.

"She will. It'll be okay."

"You tell her I'm right there with you. And if she won't let you stop doing pageants, I'm going to come down there and kick the shit out of her."

"Just come," I said.

"You know I'm kidding about kicking the shit out of her, right?"

I knew. "I just don't want anybody to be angry anymore," I said. "I want you guys to like each other."

He looked at me. "Liv—"

"All right, all right. *Get along,* then."

He hugged me again. "That's your bus," he said as the voice on the loudspeaker announced the gate.

"So? Are you coming?" I asked.

He smiled. "How about next summer? Camping at Table Rock?"

"That would be good," I said, smiling back.

When he stood up, he asked, "You all right, doing this alone?"

"Yes," I said, suddenly anxious to get on with it.

He stood with me as I waited in the line to board. I hoped that Elroy would be the driver, but the new guy's nametag said REX. Uncle Bread said to him, "This young lady is going as far as Luthers Bridge. Will you keep an eye on her, please?" which made me cringe, because I didn't want Rex thinking he was supposed to be a babysitter.

But Rex said, "Sure thing," and smiled as I climbed the stairs and found a seat by the window.

I looked down at Uncle Bread, who mouthed, "I love you, Jammie," and I rolled my eyes, but inside I was so glad. I couldn't ask him to call me the old name, but his doing it on his own was just what I wanted, exactly right.

The bus made its way south through fields of brown corn, through rain that speckled the window, through bad traffic in St. Louis and again on the interstate, past a jackknifed big rig. I thought of Daddy bleeding by the side of the road, dying alone. So many things made him come to mind. Semis in rest-stop parking lots. Telephone linemen in plaid work shirts. At the Burger King in Rolla, a man bought a plain hamburger for his little boy and it made me wonder if Daddy would have liked a boy more.

I thought, *My life is full of holes.* And also, *Do you ever get over anything?*

Late in the afternoon, when I knew she'd be out of school and at the barn, I called Imogene. She picked up on the first ring. "Oh, my God!" she said. "Where are you?"

"Coming home."

"Are you all right?"

"Yes," I said, and I could hear her breathe out, relieved.

"You've been gone, like, forever!"

"Four days."

"Yeah, but I couldn't call," she said. "It made it seem longer. I have so much to tell you!" And she launched right into her stories. She had a fight with the barn manager, who screwed up the farrier appointment. She ate lunch with Brianna Loomis, who was nice except for having some hormone problem that made her grow too much hair on her forearms. "What did you do?" she asked.

It was too much to explain all at once. "I've been in Chicago. We went to the zoo."

She laughed. "You liar."

"I'm not lying."

"There *was* a boy," she said, and I laughed, too, because it was so nice to be gotten, and also because laughing covers up crying better than just saying nothing.

We pulled into Luthers Bridge in the dark, but I could see Mama standing outside the station beneath a street lamp, her enormous shadow like a puddle at her feet. She wore an unzipped parka, and I could see her fanny pack under it, belted around her middle. I didn't see a single person in Chicago with a fanny pack. Something else from the past, like her dry, permed hair, her hot pink lipstick for special occasions.

When I stepped down off the bus, she didn't move, just stood where she was, letting me come to her. She played with the zipper on the fanny pack, giving herself something to do. When I got close, she said, "You don't know what I been through," and when I said, "I'm sorry," she grabbed me into a fierce hug and said, "Don't say you're sorry, Olivia Jane, for something so bad."

"But I am sorry," I said, crushed into her chest.

"I don't want you thinking that's enough for what you did," she said.

Even after the bus pulled away, back out to the interstate, she was still hugging me, not finished even when the attendant turned off the lamp, not caring about the cold or being alone on the empty platform.

In the car, she turned the key, and over the blast of heater air, she said, "All you're doing from now on is going to school. And coming home right after."

"I know."

"And nothing else, except Miss Denise and Mrs. Drucker."

After a minute, I said, "I'm not going to Mrs. Drucker's."

"Olivia Jane—"

"I'm not," I said.

There was a long pause. Then she said, "So you think this is how it's going to be? You telling me things and me rolling over, saying, 'That's fine, Olivia Jane'?"

"Not about everything."

I watched the town roll by: the locked-up shops, Ed's Place with its OPEN and MILLER LITE blue neon signs, the houses curtained against the night, everything ragged and small and known.

"So I suppose you think you're not doing Prettiest Doll? All that work, all that money down the drain?"

"I'm doing it. I didn't say I wasn't doing it."

"You did in your note."

I'd forgotten. "I am doing it," I said. "Not because of the money, though."

I didn't look in her direction, but I could see her smile a little, knowing she had Prettiest Doll to look forward to.

"They seen you dance a hundred times," she said. "You probably can't win if you dance."

Now I didn't say anything. Her words hung between us in the dark car, which was just starting to get warm as we pulled up to the curb at home.

sixteen

THE next two weeks were mostly a blur. I had homework to make up: French vocabulary work sheets and reading "The Ransom of Red Chief" and finding the volume of a bunch of prisms and cylinders. Mrs. Fogelson said I couldn't make up the work in her class because the kids had finished their Boston Tea Party videos. She said I could make a presentation about Chicago to the class instead.

Every day, I came home after school and practiced for the pageant: walking, twirling, smiling, posing. Remembering to make eye contact and look over my shoulder and hold my hands out and pointed down and say "Yes, ma'am" and "Thank you, ma'am."

Mama came up with practice interview questions. I answered "What do you want to be when you grow up?" and "Who is your best friend?" and "If you could spend the day doing anything at all, what would it be?" "What's your favorite subject in school?" and "What's your favorite animal?" and "If you spent the day with your mama, what would the two of you do?"

"I wouldn't make you bake cakes," Mama said after she asked me the last question. We were sitting in the kitchen while Mama unfolded the paper turkey with the accordion-pleated tail and set it in the center of the table.

"I didn't say you'd *make* me. I just figured that's what you'd want to do."

"That's what I do for fun. Myself. I wouldn't make you do the same thing I like doing unless you liked doing it, too." She crinkled up her brow, looking at the turkey, which had gotten all creased and bedraggled in the Thanksgiving box. Then she said, "Maybe *eating* cakes. Maybe we could do that together."

I laughed. It was like she was making a joke.

"See?" I said. "There's stuff we both like."

"That's what I'm telling you," she said, still looking worried, but I wasn't sure if it was still because of the turkey.

Imogene tried to be a good friend.

"You're going to win for sure," she said one day at lunch, just as the bell rang.

I balled up my paper bag and tossed it into the garbage can from where I sat on the bench. "Nothing's for sure."

"You're so pretty," she said, standing up, waiting

for me to zip my jacket. "You're not even pretty. You're beautiful."

Her saying such an extreme thing made me laugh. "No, I'm not. Not beautiful."

"You are. You didn't used to be. But you are now."

I realized I wasn't sure what the difference between pretty and beautiful is. Is beautiful just prettier than pretty? "Beautiful is too much. Beautiful is like a fabulous model or a star. It's something extra. Something you can't describe," I said. "That's not me. Pretty's enough."

"Something more than just looks," Imogene said. She sighed as we started walking toward the hallway. "You don't even get what it's like for average-looking people. What it's like to know you aren't pretty."

She sounded almost angry. I stopped walking and put my hand on her arm. "I didn't think you cared about what you look like," I said.

She jerked her arm away. "Of course I care, Liv. Everyone cares. How can I not care?" We started walking again. "When it's all anybody thinks about."

"You don't wear cute clothes or makeup. Not even lip gloss."

"What's the point? What difference would it make?"

"I could teach you how to do it. So it would make a difference. There are things you can do. Tricks."

"Like what?"

"Like when you put on mascara. The stuff to make your eyelashes look long," I added, because I wasn't sure she knew what it was. "Before you put it on, dust a little powder on your lashes. It makes them look thicker. And for your lips, a cream lipstick with a shimmer will kind of perk up your skin."

"I wouldn't want to be too shiny."

"Then you can use a beige or light brown top coat. Just a little. There are all kinds of things you can do."

"How do you know all this stuff?" she asked.

"The same way you know about horses. Being around it so long. You just learn it. All the tricks." We split apart to walk around a clump of seventh grade boys. Back together, I said, "It's all just tricks."

"I don't know how you remember it," Imogene said. "It just kind of leaks out of my head."

"Because you don't care. Not really," I said when she started to argue. "You think you do, but you don't. Not in the way that counts."

"It feels like caring when I look in the mirror and see this drab, plain girl looking back," she said, shrugging but not mad anymore.

"Not plain," I said, turning to head down the other hall to French. "Beautiful."

She kept walking, but I turned around and saw her laughing.

"Really!" I yelled, and she looked back, smiling, so I know she'd heard.

whazzup? Dan IMed me that night.

doing homework, I IMed back.

We talked like this almost every night. Totally unromantic. It was okay. I figured there were two ways to go with someone like Dan: either I could be sad and pine away for him, or I could force myself to think of him as just a friend. Without even talking about it, that was what we'd both decided to do: force ourselves to be friends.

i wish u had skype, he said.

the webcams r too expensive

well save up for one then

i might, I said.

I sighed. The problem with just being friends was that there was too much feeling all locked away, so all that was left was boring, barely-knowing-a-person conversation. I couldn't think of much to say to him that wouldn't let all the locked-away feelings loose.

Then he IMed, *got my first shot,* and I felt everything flood through me.

did it hurt? I asked.

ya. i have to have them every day. ☹

are you sorry? I asked.

not really

That's good, I said. Back to the barely-knowing-him stuff.

I was trying to remember the French word for *peach* when he typed, *sometimes it feels weird to admit that i care what i look like.*

I put my hands up to type an answer, then set them in my lap. I thought for a long time. Finally, I typed, *look who youre telling this to.*

You're the only one I've told, he said. *lol*

Why? I asked.

He said, *because thinking about what you look like all the time is not so different from not thinking about it at all.*

deep, I wrote, just to be funny. But my hands were shaking a little.

so how much did you practice today? He meant for the pageant.

2 hours

sad day

it was ok. miss denise said maybe the break did me some good. she says my smile is better

He didn't answer for a long time. I was looking up *asparagus* in my English-French dictionary when he typed, *What did she say about the singing?*

that its still bad. Terrible. lol

I'd finished the last of my French when I realized he'd left me a last IM. All it said was *your smile is amazing*.

Mama and I drove to Jefferson City on the Friday before Thanksgiving. We pulled into the hotel driveway after dark. "Look at all the twinkly lights," Mama said. "Ain't this pretty?" She was always like that in front of hotels: bowled over by the lights, the luggage racks on wheels, the parking valets smoking cigarettes off to the side of the building, where the people in the front lobby couldn't see. I think she was just amazed to be in a place where someone else made the beds and cleaned the toilet. That was enough to make it grand.

"Pretty," I said.

"Olivia Jane, you sound tired," she said as we got out of the car and hurried, shivering, into the lobby. "We got to get to sleep early. Hair and makeup's at seven."

Mama was right. I was tired in my bones. I stood next to her while she gave the check-in clerk our reservation number and thought that all I wanted to do was lie on cool white sheets and watch cop shows in the dark, which was something special that Mama had just started allowing on pageant nights.

The check-in clerk was a dark-haired woman, not very old, fat enough so she didn't have wrists. She wore the hotel company's uniform, but she'd decorated the blouse with bird pins. I counted twelve, all with cheap, glittery stones for eyes. "I like your pins," Mama said.

The woman smiled. "It's a hobby of mine."

"Birds?" Mama asked. I knew she was getting ready to tell about Grandpa's taxidermy business.

"No. Pins. Collecting them." She handed Mama the credit card bill and a pen. "I like birds well enough, though." She looked at me. "They let you wear pins on your pretty pageant clothes?"

"Probably not," I said.

The woman sighed and shook her head. "You're lucky, being so pretty. Being in pageants. I bet you won a lot of 'em, huh?"

"A couple," I said.

Mama laughed. "Oh, she's just being modest. She's won a bunch. How many, Olivia Jane?" Without waiting for me to answer, she said, "Twenty-three, I think. Twenty-three she actually *won.* That's not counting all the ones she come in first runner-up."

"Mama."

The woman laughed. "It's okay, honey. Your mama's *proud.* Let her be proud."

"Well, now, that's what I say." Mama folded the receipt and put it in her wallet, then snapped her big purse shut. "But a lot of people say it's a bad thing being so proud. Say us moms are *pushy*. Say we should just keep our mouths shut, pretend not to notice."

"I know. I *know*. It's a thankless job!" The woman shook her head, commiserating with Mama. "Well, I say good for you. Good for you both." She looked right at me. "I'll be rooting for you," she said. Then she leaned over the counter and whispered, "You're the prettiest one so far!"

"Well, now, wasn't she sweet?" Mama said as we turned away from the desk and headed back outside to park the car. The automatic door whooshed open, and the bellboy, bored and pimply, looked us up and down. He smiled at me and looked away, the way eighteen-year-old boys often do, not sure whether being so much older made him look good to me or if he seemed creepy and sad for even thinking about smiling at a girl so young.

"Mama," I said as she started the car and drove slowly into the crowded parking lot, "if I didn't do pageants, would you be proud of me?"

"Well, now, for Lord's sake, what kind of a question is that?"

"Would you be proud of me?"

"Well, of course I would." She was squinting and hunching forward over the steering wheel, straining to see in the dark.

"For what?"

"Olivia Jane. I am too tired to play this game."

"It's not a game," I said, but I didn't say anything more until she had eased the car into place and turned off the engine. "Okay, now. What would you be proud of me for?"

She just sat for a minute, her thick hands still on the wheel. Finally she said, "I don't know."

I looked out the window at the battered SUV next to us. Through its passenger window I could see two baby car seats and, in the back, a cardboard box with CLEANING SUPPLIES written across the top flap. Were the babies in the pageant? Was the mama a maid who carried her work things around so she wouldn't forget them for a job? Did the daddy come along, happy to carry the suitcase because the mama had both babies to get in and out of the car? Were they proud of those babies? Weren't they supposed to be? Wasn't that their job?

"You been doing pageants for a long time," Mama said. "I got used to being proud of you for that. I ain't gonna apologize."

We sat, our breathing fogging up the windows.

"But if there was other stuff you did . . ." She sighed. "I don't know *what*. But if there was, I'd probably figure out something to . . . I don't know. *Like,* I guess. But I don't want you thinking that means I'm saying it's okay to give up on pageants. Because it's not."

"I'm not thinking that."

"They're so good for you, Olivia Jane. The way they make you confident. The way you walk into a room and just, I don't know, know you belong there. I could never do that," she said sadly.

"Yes," I said. "I can do that."

"It's a gift you got, the way you look. A gift. And you know, them people who say it's not right for girls to think so much about how they look, they're living in some kind of dreamland if they think that's not what girls do anyway, And not just girls. Grown women, too. It's what we do. It's everything." She looked at me. "And you're just so pretty. So pretty. And I ain't gonna say I'm sorry about that, or that it's a bad thing."

"It's not a bad thing. But—"

"No. No buts." She turned back to the steering wheel and pulled the key out of the ignition. "Olivia Jane, we got to get up to the room. I am way too tired to do any more talking."

"Me, too. I'm tired, too."

"And you know we got an early start tomorrow." She pulled herself out of the car and up to standing. She looked at me over the roof. "How 'bout a little TV tonight, honey?" she said.

"Okay," I said, taking what she could give me.

"And maybe a milk shake if the coffee shop's still open," she said, pulling our suitcase out of the trunk. "How's that sound?"

I nodded, knowing that, even if I said no, she'd order two in case I changed my mind and wait until I fell asleep to drink them both.

seventeen

THAT night, I couldn't sleep. I lay alone in the bed closest to the window, listening to Mama snore. We'd turned the TV off hours ago and left the curtains open. The nighttime was yellow with parking-lot light. Jefferson City was asleep. No sound except, once in a while, a semi out on the highway, making me think the same old thoughts, making me tired, but not enough to sleep. Weary. Tired in my head.

Even the hotel was silent. Usually at hotels with conference rooms there are people in the halls at all hours, stumbling around, laughing and whispering. They aren't pageant people. They're businesspeople who've stayed up late, drinking. The pageant people are always in their rooms early, the girls asleep, the moms fretting, trying to remember if they've packed the extra Magic Tan, if there'll be enough time in the morning to iron the baton-twirling costume again. Pageant moms can always think of one more thing that needs doing.

That bird-pin lady at the front desk had looked all

admiringly at Mama, thinking how hard she'd worked, but she didn't know the half of it, what Mama does. So much. There's always something last-minute to remember, another fake nail to paint, another sequin to sew on.

The bird-pin lady got to go home and stop thinking about her day at the reservations desk. Or maybe she thought about it, but there wasn't anything more to *do*. She could watch TV, knit a baby blanket, tell her husband about the businessman who'd dug around in the outdoor trash bins looking for something and left trash all over the parking lot. That had really happened once. I was nine. I heard the clerk say, "But, sir, you're on the surveillance video," and the man say, "What is this, CIA headquarters? I want to talk to your supervisor!"

Maybe I slept a little. When I looked over at the alarm clock on the bedside table, it was 4:13. I stared straight up into the blackness, straining to hear sounds from the conference room at the end of the hall. Sometimes the workers start early, setting up chairs, hanging banners, putting the trophies out on a table so all the girls will know what they're shooting for, what's at stake.

But I heard nothing. It reminded me of Dan's father's house, vast and hushed in the early morning, Dan's half brother and half sister standing silently in front of their closets, choosing clothes for school, Suzy Jacobson pouring coffee, anxious to get to the barn, where the horses snorted and pawed the dirt, waiting. All those rooms, and no one talking.

The blackness swirled and I started to fall and right before I felt it wrap its arms around me I had the funniest thought, that if Mama didn't have pageants to think about, there might be nothing else in her head.

"Olivia Jane," she whispered. "Come on, honey. It's pageant day."

I groaned. I think I said, "I'm not doing this."

"Come on, honey," Mama said, not in a whisper now. "Up and at 'em. Let's get ready to rumble," which is what she always says.

I forced myself up to sitting, my hair a mess around my face, my face still hot from sleep.

"Your interview's at eight, and Miss Denise will be here any minute," Mama said. "Come on. Brush your teeth and wash your face. And then put your gown on."

"I gotta pee first," I said grumpily and slammed the bathroom door.

A few minutes later, I sat on the closed toilet lid and watched myself in the mirror as Mama set my hair in hot rollers. I was wearing my burgundy gown, still warm from the ironing Mama had given it on the fold-out board in the wall by the door. I had a big towel over my shoulders like a stole, to make sure the dress didn't get wet or stained.

"Ouch!" I said as she jabbed a bobby pin into my scalp. *"Ouch!"*

"Hush!" Mama said. "Don't be a baby." She worked fast, prying each pin apart with her teeth before sliding it in place.

When she was finished, I couldn't help laughing. "I look like Marie Antoinette in her wig."

"Who?" Mama said, not really paying attention. She stared fiercely at the snowy folds of my skirt. "You think I got all the wrinkles out?" she said, but before I could answer, there was a knock at the door and we heard Miss Denise half whispering out in the hall, "It's me, Janie!"

She was wearing black jeans and a bright green blazer and too much perfume, the kind some movie star makes, because if you're a movie star, then you know what men like. At least, that's what Miss Denise says. "Well, good Lord, girl!" she said, squeezing herself into the tiny bathroom with me. "Don't you just look *fantastic!*"

"Thanks," I said.

"Ooh, Janie, this dress is perfect. *Per-fect.* It sets off her skin so *nice.*" Miss Denise put her makeup cases on the counter and looked me up and down, hands on her hips. "Oh, yes. Perfect. Don't you think, Olivia?"

"I think it'll make the judges think of Christmas," I said.

"Oh, yes. Definitely. Yes, indeed," Miss Denise said, nodding, still judging. "You'll knock their socks off."

"That's what I think," Mama said from the doorway. "You don't think it looks wrinkled?"

"I don't think so, Janie, no." Miss Denise studied every part of me as though I was a car she was thinking of buying, then flashed her pageant smile at Mama. "You did good, girl!"

Mama smiled. "I was worrying all night about wrinkles," she said.

"Now, Olivia, you haven't eaten this morning, have you?" Miss Denise unzipped one of her cases, getting ready for makeup applicating. "You don't want to be looking puffy onstage."

Something changed on Mama's face. "Denise, I'm not one for having Olivia Jane skip meals."

"I'm just saying—"

Mama's brow furrowed. "In our house, we don't believe in not eating for no good reason."

Mama had been a yo-yo dieter when she was a girl. She knew how bad that was.

Miss Denise shrugged in a suit-yourself kind of

way, and also in a well-I'm-too-polite-to-say-so-but-have-you-looked-in-a-mirror-lately? kind of way. My heart broke a little, but Mama ignored her. She pulled an apple and a cruller and a plastic bottle of orange juice from her suitcase and handed them to me. "Here you go, baby," she said.

I took a huge bite of the apple and chewed loudly on purpose. It tasted absolutely delicious.

Miss Denise fussed with her makeup brushes, pretending to ignore me. "How much time we got, Janie? Half hour? Forty minutes?" She looked at me, suddenly all business, and said, "Let's get a move on, Olivia. We're running out of time."

I finished my breakfast while Miss Denise arranged her brushes and creams and gels and powders. Foundation and concealer, eyelash curler, false eyelashes, liner. Like at the dentist's office: all the tools for poking and scraping laid out. I raised my face to the light so Miss Denise could see her work.

She told me when to close my eyes, when to look up, when to purse my lips. Her eyes narrowed into slits. I knew it wasn't really me she was seeing. By the end, I would be invisible, hidden away.

"You been practicing your dance?" she asked. Wanting to let me know how mad she was about Mrs. Drucker, all the trouble she'd gone through to get me a lesson, how ungrateful I was, and full of myself, turning up my nose at that kind of opportunity.

"I'm not dancing," I said. "I'm singing."

Miss Denise's jaw dropped. She looked up at Mama, who was standing behind me in the tub, taking the rollers out of my hair. Then she looked back at me.

"What? Olivia Jane, are you out of your gol-darned mind?" she said.

"I'm doing it."

"You been practicing? On your own? Janie, did you know about this?"

Mama shook her head as she fumbled with a roller, her lips folded into a thin, stiff line. "I did not. And I ain't too happy about it, neither."

"Well, I can see why." Miss Denise glared at me. "Olivia, I am taken aback by this."

"It's all right," I said. "It'll be all right."

"Honey, have you heard yourself?" She shook her head. "I don't understand why you didn't go see Mrs. Elsie Drucker if you had your heart set on singing."

"It will be all right," I said.

In the mirror, I could see Miss Denise and Mama exchange a look. Mama shook her head and said, "I guess it's in the Lord's hands now," and Miss Denise, who didn't care for church, said, "I hope He's wearing earplugs."

Minutes later, I was finished. Looking at myself in the mirror in my gown, my hair-sprayed curls tumbling over my shoulders, my face shiny with new glaze, I smiled.

Mama stood behind me, her eyes going a little misty. "So pretty, huh?"

"Yes," I said, but that wasn't why I was smiling.

It was because, for the first time, I could see myself under all that stuff.

We walked fast down the hallway toward the conference room. "Good luck!" the woman sitting at the table out front whispered after she'd checked me in.

Mama put her hands on my arms. "Now you just do your best, honey," she said. "Remember everything we talked about. I'll be praying for you."

Miss Denise pointed to my eyes, then to hers, then back to mine. "Eye contact. *Eye contact.* And smile," she said.

I nodded, already not listening, going into myself. "I know," I said.

I waited until they'd gone in, then hurried down another hall to get to the door at the front of the conference room, where they'd set up the stage. The carpet was blue with swirls of gold dots, like galaxies of stars in space. Two little girls—blond, in sparkly dresses—stood by the wall, watched over by their mothers. "I'm gonna win!" the taller one said, nodding her head so hard that she tipped at the waist. "I'm gonna win, too!" the other one said, but quietly, not nodding. The taller one glared at her. "Winning only counts if there's just one," she said. One of the women leaned down and whispered, "Chantilly, you hush!"

At the door, a woman wearing a red dress and a headset stood with a clipboard. "Olivia Jane Tatum?" she asked. "You ready for your interview, honey?"

"Yes, ma'am."

"It'll be another minute. Amber Dickerson's just finishing up. I'm Donna, by the way. I'm Mrs. Crosby's assistant." She folded her arms across the clipboard, clamping it to her chest. "You done many pageants?" she asked. "You look like you done a lot of them."

"I've done a few."

"You girls all look so pretty. The little ones"—she glanced at Chantilly and her friend down the hall—"they're all so cute. But you older girls. Well, now you can really see. You know. The ones who've stuck with it this long, well, you're the pretty ones. The ones who'll be pretty grownups." She opened the door and peeked in, then closed it, holding the handle so the latch wouldn't make a loud click. "The ones who give up on it have to find another hobby, I guess," she said.

"It's not a hobby, exactly."

"Oh, you're *right.* It's a *lifestyle,* isn't it?" She smiled. "You ever met Mrs. Crosby?"

Mrs. Crosby was the pageant coordinator. I'd seen her at the registration desk the night before. She had black hair except for a stripe of silver on the right side, flipped up at the ends. "Just last night," I said.

"She's so *nice.* She loves all you girls. She used to be a schoolteacher. Second grade, I think. But she wanted to do something more. And she was tired of the boys. The way they couldn't sit still." She peeked into the conference room again. "Amber's almost done. You ready, honey?"

"Yes, ma'am. I think so."

"Now just relax. Have fun with it. And smile." She laughed. "I guess you know that, right?"

The door opened and Amber Dickerson flounced between us. She wore pale pink, and her creamy, sun-tanned skin sparkled with body glitter. "Stupid question!" she said. "Damn!" She looked angrily at Donna, ready to argue if she said anything about watching her language. But Donna just smiled nervously and checked something off on her clipboard.

"What'd they ask you?" I asked.

"If I were stuck on an island in the middle of the ocean, what would I bring? Like, how many times have

I answered *that* one? Is my hair okay?" she asked, puffing it up with her gloved hands.

"It's fine. What did you say?" I asked, only half-listening, waiting to hear my name announced.

"I don't know. A picture of my granny. A book. I don't know." She shook her head. "Shit. I should have said a Bible. Shit."

"Olivia Jane, you're on," Donna said, holding one hand to her headset and pushing me gently through the door. "Good luck!" I heard her whisper.

Out onstage, I felt myself smiling, holding my hands stiffly down at my sides, my head tall on my neck. I didn't even have to think. The parts of my body that had work to do just did it, without my even trying. I glanced out at the room, which, I could see now, was just a room, with rows of metal folding chairs, most of them not even being sat on. When I was little, I thought conference rooms looked like movie theaters, grand, the rows of seats extending back and back.

A few parents were clustered up near the front. Mama and Miss Denise were craning their necks, as if there were people in front of them they had to struggle to see over. I looked carefully for the judges' table, finding it in the front, just at the end of the stage and its little makeshift runway. Three judges, a man and two women. I knew the man and one of the women from other pageants. The women were in their thirties, both wearing the kind of sparkly, low-cut dresses that you're supposed to wear at night. The man was African American and wore a gray pinstriped suit with a blue satin handkerchief in the breast pocket.

Mrs. Crosby, holding a clipboard in one hand and a microphone in the other, stood in the center of the stage, waiting for me. Her face was lit with a schoolteachery smile that said "Relax, dear" and "Get your fanny out here right now" at the same time. "Olivia Jane Tatum!" she said into the microphone. I heard scattered applause, Mama clapping hard, Miss Denise calling, "You go, girl!" I smiled big at each judge, meeting each one's eyes. The skirt of my dress bobbled stiffly as I walked.

I reached the center of the stage, and Mrs. Crosby said, "Well, now, Olivia." She smiled as she looked out at the audience. "Your question is, 'Who do you admire most, and why?' " Standing next to her, I thought she seemed to be made of porcelain or clay: something that would break if you dropped it. She was too thin for a grown lady. The silver stripe in her hair made me think that her forehead should have had lines in it.

I thought for a moment. Then I said, "The person I admire most is my friend Dan, because he gets teased all the time for something he can't help. And even though he hates being teased, he doesn't let that make him stop being who he really is."

I could see Miss Denise wincing. She would have said that I was making it too complicated, that I should have kept things simple and just said my mom.

"This Daniel sounds like quite a young man," Mrs. Crosby said. "Is he a classmate of yours?"

"No. Just a friend. He has to do something hard that he doesn't really want to do. But he's going to do it anyway, for his mama, and maybe a little bit for himself." I'd said too much. I'd gotten too serious. I was making Mrs. Crosby nervous. I knew she wanted the next girl to come out. But I kept talking. "He taught me that part of growing up is knowing when to stand up for yourself. And that, sometimes, backing down is the right thing to do, the better path to walk."

Mrs. Crosby didn't know what to do with that. "Thank you, Olivia Jane Tatum!" she said into her microphone. I knew she was just praying that that would get me to shut up and give the next girl a turn.

Before I turned to make my way backstage, I saw one of the judges lean over her scorecard and make a check mark. When she looked up again, she smiled at me and winked.

"How'd you do?" Donna said when I'd gotten back out into the hallway.

"Okay. Not so great, maybe. I don't know." My heart was thudding.

"It's hard to tell sometimes." She patted my glove. "Don't worry, honey. You just get yourself back down here at eleven for Talent, okay?"

Mama and Miss Denise were heading toward me. "Who's this Dan?" Mama was asking as Miss Denise said, "It's okay, it's okay. It's just Interview. We got lots of time. Don't nobody panic."

I let them fuss for a minute, primping my curls, smoothing my skirt. Mama asked Miss Denise was I better than the others, and Miss Denise said it didn't matter, I was prettier than any of the other gol-darned girls.

I didn't say anything. I thought how just talking about him—saying his name—made it seem like he was in the room with me.

I wore my green satin dress for Talent. "It's cute," Miss Denise said as she and Mama rode the elevator down with me, Miss Denise taking advantage of the privacy to floss her teeth. "They'll see you got cute legs." She wrapped the used floss around her fingers and stuffed it in her purse.

Outside the stage door, I let Donna tell me what everyone else was doing: Amber was tap dancing, Candace Hebert was twirling a baton, Whitney Sullivan was doing a cheerleading routine with cartwheels and splits. A few girls were singing. Marla Timmons had sung "My Heart Will Go On" like an opera singer. I'd heard her sing it before. It gave me goose bumps.

"You all set?" Donna asked me as McKenzie French left the stage after doing gymnastics to "Cowboy Casanova."

"Yes, ma'am," I said, but my teeth were chattering.

"Let's welcome back Olivia Jane Tatum!" Mrs. Crosby said from the stage. I felt Donna's push on my back and walked out into the bright lights and the clapping that sounded like wild animals scrabbling in an attic. I smiled from habit. I reached the center of the stage and beamed at each judge, but only because I was so used to doing it that I did it automatically, without thinking.

I was vibrating with fear.

Oh! You beautiful doll,
You great big beautiful doll!
Let me put my arms about you,
I could never live without you;

Oh! You beautiful doll,
You great big beautiful doll!

I was terrible. I could tell. But somehow, it was all right, better than if I'd tried to prop myself up with lessons from Mrs. Drucker, who wouldn't have made a difference in just a week or two. That would have been something I did for Mama and Miss Denise. This was just for me, to show myself I could.

It was weird not to mind being bad at something, for once.

If you ever leave me, how my heart will ache,
I want to hug you but I fear you'd break.

Oh, oh, oh, oh,
Oh, you beautiful doll!
Oh, oh, oh, oh,
Oh, you beautiful doll!

If I was going to spend time working at getting good at something, it wasn't going to be singing. Chess, maybe, or public speaking. Mrs. Fogelson would sponsor a public-speaking club, I was pretty sure. The pretty girls and the jocks would laugh. It was okay. I could be in my own box.

The judges were writing things down, whispering to each other. Mrs. Crosby, standing off to the side, bit her lower lip and looked out at the audience, smiling a little, as though she was saying she was sorry and not to worry, it would be over soon.

The applause was thin; Miss Denise's "You go, Olivia Jane!" was too loud and made the clapping sound even quieter.

I smiled and bowed, happiness and maybe just a little relief flooding through me like a river.

Beauty was at two o'clock. The babies were first, held up by their mamas for the judges to see. I stood at the back of the conference room with all the girls from the preteen and teen divisions to watch. It was always my favorite part of any pageant. The babies were so cute in their little suits, and the mamas so proud and each sure her own particular baby would win.

The Pee Wees were next. Pushed out onstage by their mamas, who got to stand backstage with them. Some of the girls cried; one stamped her foot and sat down on the stage, pouting. The people in the audience laughed, knowing it was always a risk, that a little girl might just throw a fit for the whole dang world to see. The girl sitting down let her mama pull her up to standing, but when she stamped her foot again, her mama led her off. The other mamas clapped politely and said things to each other about how hard it is to miss a nap. But I could tell they were faking their niceness. They were really thinking, *My daughter's so much better. My daughter's going to win.*

The Little Misses were between five and seven, so their mamas stood in the back of the room, reminding them what they were supposed to be doing. They pointed at their own teeth-baring smiles and mouthed "Look at the judges!" without actually talking. The girls smiled and turned, and one of them—so happy to be the center of everyone's attention—even waved as she walked offstage. Their faces were all pretty, all a little bit the same: a painted-on blankness, smiles that had been learned, nothing to do with happiness. Eyes propped open, unblinking.

We—the teens—were next. Lining up outside the door, I smiled, thinking of what everyone would do if I just sat down on the stage and refused to move. Of course, I wouldn't really do it. But in the old days, I wouldn't even have let myself think about it: it would have been like standing too close to the edge of the Grand Canyon and feeling as though you might forget yourself and jump. Now I didn't care. Now I thought, *I could if I wanted.*

"Your singing sucked," Amber Dickerson whispered. She was just ahead of me, in her cotton candy dress, leaning backwards to whisper so Donna couldn't hear.

"I know," I said.

"My coach said they might make a new rule, that you're not allowed to sing unless you get pageant-director approval first. All because of you," Amber said.

"It's okay," I said.

"They'll probably call it the Olivia Jane Tatum Rule."

"Maybe they will," I said. And when she looked shocked, I added, "Now, why don't you just shut your dang mouth and *go?*"

It took her a moment to realize that she'd almost missed her cue. I could tell from the way she began to walk that I'd addled her, that she wasn't thinking about walking. Which, I knew from Miss Denise, is half the battle, the most important thing.

But when it was my turn, I didn't need to think, or take a breath, or anything. I felt as though I had no legs or arms, no separate parts that had to be told where to go and what to do. It was different from all the other times, when my smile felt painted on and all that was in my head was winning. Now I floated in my snow-white skirt, inches above the stage and the rickety cat-walk, gliding, winged, a tulle-draped angel. I turned like swirling stars in space. I smiled, not even worrying how much gum I showed. And I knew, from the way the judges were smiling back, that it was in my eyes, and that they could see it, that they knew the difference.

★

Later, standing with the other preteens onstage, waiting while Mrs. Crosby fumbled with her microphone, I looked out into the audience, searching for Mama. She was sitting next to Miss Denise, straining to hear, clutching her hands in her lap. "Smile!" she mouthed, and then, "You're so beautiful."

Amber got second runner-up; Candace Hebert got first, a surprise: she usually got fourth or fifth. Her mama and daddy stood up and clapped as Mrs. Crosby handed Candace her trophy. I clapped, too, happy for her, thinking she had worked so hard and so long, glad she had been recognized. The best thing was, finally, to be seen.

There was a moment of silence, drawn out by Mrs. Crosby, after "And the Prettiest Doll is . . ." I thought it would be one of those moments when everything changes—where you are one way on one side and another way on the other—but it wasn't. It was just a moment.

Even so, I realized a lot of things in that second of silence: that I had won, that I didn't need a crown to tell me what I already knew.

That Mama would be crushed when I told her I was through with pageants for good, that she would yell and cry and sulk and it wouldn't change my mind.

That somehow she would get used to being proud of me for other things. Maybe public speaking. Maybe something I didn't even know I was good at yet.

That my daddy was watching it all from somewhere. That he was proud enough to burst. That if he were around, he would be telling me I had a smile that could light up Heaven.

And that I'd tell Dan tonight and he'd ask me how the singing went. And when I said terrible, he would sigh and say, *its too bad you couldnt challenge those judges to a game of chess because thatd show them.* And then he would say, *i cant believe you did that stupid thing.* And maybe it would piss me off and maybe it wouldn't, but I'd tell him either way.